I0687104

TRUST
HONOR
LOVE

BLIND VOWS
VOLUME 1

BY: J.M. WITT

Copyright 2015 © J.M. Witt

Cover Artist: Sommer Stein
Photographer: Darren Birks Photography
Model: Anne Ransom
Editor: Leticia Sidon
Publisher: J.M. Witt Books

All Rights Reserved 2015

This book may not be reproduced in any form; in whole or in part, without written permission by the author.

All characters and events in this book are fictional. Any similarities to real life people and events are purely coincidental.

Copyright © 2015 J.M. Witt

All Rights Reserved 2015

ISBN: 978-0692470572

DEDICATED TO TYF SNYDER

DON'T STOP FIGHTING,
WRITING, DREAMING,
OR BEING YOU.

#FIGHTASAFAMILY
#EFFCANCER

ACKNOWLEDGMENTS

Thank you to everyone who's read my work and continues to do so. This project took me by surprise and I've loved every minute of it.

First, I have to thank Darren Birks for being such a pleasure to work with. This story hit me and when I told you my vision for the cover, you were nothing but supportive. Thank you. You also make an amazing muse for my Heathcliff and FitzWilliam!

Anne, your picture seriously haunted me. I'm so happy to have you on the first cover for this series. Thank you for being my Lucy!

Teri F. You know what you did. Thank you!

Rebecca, Betsy, and Leticia. WOW. You three were bombarded with this secret project and took off running with me. Thank you for your overwhelming support and belief. Words will never be enough to express what it means to me.

Tami, Tracey, and Elaine. Three more of the most supportive fans and friends a girl could ever ask for. Thank you!

Stacey and Jaime: Well, what else is there to say, but 'Give the man some head!'

Tyf and Skye. There are no words for me to say. Your friendship means the world to me. I never would've made it this far without you two. I love you dearly.

To my friends and family. Thank you for your support. You know who you are!

TABLE OF CONTENTS

TABLE OF CONTENTS CONT.

Love

TRUST

~ PROLOGUE ~

~ LUCY ~

The head and heart are pretty good at getting tangled up in one another, especially when love is involved. The day my life changed wasn't linked to just one particular event. It all started six months prior with an unexpected encounter. I never anticipated that the chain of events that would follow would lead me to where I was today and that they were all linked. But, that's life for you, right? Fate, divine intervention, the cosmos, whatever you call it or believe in, it was still all a little unfathomable to me. It also taught me to never say never and to explore all the possibilities.

~ CHAPTER 1 ~

~ LUCY ~

Another horrid date to add to my list of epic fails. I was so sick of the dating websites. Where did these guys come from? I grabbed my cell and called Stacey. Odds were that she was out or headed home from work. It wasn't too late to join her and salvage my night. As I suspected, she was on her way home and to our favorite bar just down the street. Grabbing my clutch, I walked the short distance. It wasn't yet dark, another reminder at how early my date had ended.

I was living alone and had been for almost two years. Stacey and I knew enough about each other to know while we were great friends, we'd make horrible roommates. So, instead, we both had one bedroom apartments in the same building. It was the next best thing.

I sighed heavily as I walked into the restaurant and grabbed a table, waiting for Stacey to arrive. I went ahead and ordered our drinks and shortly after the waitress set them down, Stacey walked in. Sitting down, I could tell she was immediately annoyed. There were only two possibilities; her boss or her ex. My money was on her boss.

"I *have* to find a new job!" Ding, ding, ding.

"You've been saying that for months. What's stopping you?"

Sighing, she agreed, "I know. I just hate change." She took a sip of her drink and then asked me, "What about you? Anything new going on?"

"Eh, another douche to add to the list."

"That good, huh?"

"You could say that."

"He's out there. And he better have a friend for me!" I caught her staring at the bar and I followed the nod of her head. "I don't know why you don't just date one of the Kerry boys. You can't go wrong with any of them."

What was *he* doing here? "Ugh. Yes, I can…Go wrong! And it's Kerrigan, not Kerry."

"Kerry, Kerrigan, whatever. How in the world did two people have such different sons? NONE of them look alike, well, except for the twins."

"Maybe some of her students fathered them, or maybe the mailman!"

Stacey started cracking up and I joined her as we joked about the possibility of each son being fathered by someone different. Mrs. Kerrigan was an English Lit professor and had some odd quirks, but she was also very attractive, as was her husband.

"Well, it's probably for the best. Means I can have my pick of the Kerrigan boys."

"Umm, they're all yours."

It was a busy Friday night and Stacey and I could sense how annoyed our waitress was getting with us. If she wasn't careful she would lose her tip. We had no plans of leaving anytime soon and finally ordered food after an hour of occupying our booth and drinking. The lights dimmed shortly after our food arrived and the last few families that were present paid their tabs and left. The music grew louder and people started filling the bar.

Taking a bite of my burger, his voice grated through me, like nails on a chalkboard. Stacey heard him, too. His boisterous, over-cocky, sex-filled voice, full of gravel. I was sure everyone in the bar heard him, the way he liked it. Clamping my legs together, trying to ignore my body's reaction to his voice, I chewed my food a little more vigorously than necessary, which resulted in me biting my cheek.

"Ugh." Placing my burger back to the plate, I massaged my cheek as Stacey and I exchanged nods. Time to finish our food and get the hell out of there before he spotted us. He hadn't spotted me yet, and if he had, he was doing a great job of ignoring me.

When we finished eating, I offered to pay the bill and Stacey objected. "No way. After that wretched date, my treat." We both laughed and downed the remainder of our drinks. Anxiously awaiting the waitress, and Stacey's credit card, I spotted him walking over.

"Fuck!" I recognized *Hollow Moon* by AWOLNATION as it droned overhead. It was as if he was strolling along to the beat and everything started moving in slow motion, like some movie out of the 80's or 90's where the underrated good girl spotted the bad boy who was headed her way.

Fucking Heathcliff Kerrigan.

Though everyone called him Heath for short. And he alone was the bane of my existence. Over six feet tall, he was sex on legs. With a hand in his pocket, the other ran through his shaggy hair, hair that was cropped close on the sides, but was long on top—the best of both worlds. The slick strands matched the color of his eyes, when not covered in gel. He pushed those dark strands aside, revealing his eyes; chocolate saucers that pulled you into their depths without even trying. A short beard covered a face so perfectly sculpted that it should be a crime. He wore a button-up shirt, unbuttoned on top, exposing just enough chest to make any hot blooded woman's fingers itch. His sleeves were rolled up, exposing his muscled forearms, and then his jeans... Jeans that looked like they were tailored specifically for him. And yes, I wanted to see what he had packing underneath his well-fit clothes and I hated myself for it.

"Lucy, Lucy, Lucy. I thought that was you sitting over here." I closed my eyes, trying to ignore the throb between my legs that had started the minute I saw him. Such a waste of man, sexy voice with a body to match, but the brain of an egomaniac. He was hot and he knew it. "All alone on a Friday night or you still pining away for me?"

"Aren't you sweet?" I couldn't bear to make eye contact with him—with those eyes that screamed 'Fuck me'—and assumed he caught my sarcastic tone. "Believe it or not, I'm not pining. Pining would mean that I cared in the first place, Heath."

"Right, if I was William it'd be a different story." That caught my attention. He knew I had a soft spot for his twin brother, always had. "You know, to this day you're still the only one who can consistently tell us apart? We can still fool our parents if we really want to."

I didn't need the reminder of why it was I was the one able to tell them apart. "Maybe because your mother's books are more appealing than you are?" He narrowed his eyes at me as I continued. "You can't fool me. Your hair is always a mess, too cocky for your own good, you never shave, and you will sleep with just about anything that walks. Well, as long as she's not too brainy. I know how smart chicks dampen..." I looked to his crotch, "...things. And not in a good way."

Stacey snorted, her laughter filling the small space between us all as Heath continued to stare me down.

He clutched his heart, like he was wounded. "Ouch."

I could feel his eyes drilling into the side of my face, willing me to dare make eye contact once more. *Don't look, don't look.* If I made eye contact, surely I'd be turned to stone, like Medusa did to her victims. Heath was my Medusa. I focused on every other part of him, doing everything I could to avoid his eyes.

The waitress placed down two more drinks as Stacey and I objected.

"Drinks are on me tonight." I looked to Heath, back to Stacey and then to Heath again. The waitress handed Stacey her credit card and receipt before walking away. "No need to say thank you." He winked and walked away before I could say anything in return.

I felt like a total jerk. "That was awkward." I glanced at Stacey, not sure how to reply. She pushed my drink toward me and took a swig of her own. "Might as well stay if he's buying our drinks."

"I don't think that's what he meant, Stacey."

Laughing she said, "Well, that's the impression I got. Bottoms up!"

A few hours later we were continuing to run up Heath's tab. If he knew what we were doing he wasn't objecting. Deciding to leave, Stacey and I weaved our arms together, stumbling toward the exit when Heath appeared out of nowhere, blocking the exit.

"You ladies aren't driving."

Grinning like a fool I chirped, "No worries. I walked." I tried to push past him when he put his hands on my shoulders.

"Lucy, you're not walking either. You can barely stand."

Rolling my eyes, I slurred, "Suit yourself," I motioned toward the closed door as Stacey and I waited for him to open it.

"Hey! Your tab." The waitress ran toward us as Stacey and I scurried out the door Heath had pushed open.

"Thanks for the drinks Heath." He glared after me before ultimately heading back in to deal with the tab, allowing my escape.

~ CHAPTER 2 ~

~ LUCY ~

Stacey and I were half a block away when Heath jumped in front of us again and put his hands up to stop us. "That was slick of you. Kudos. You two just rang up over fifty dollars in drinks."

"Is that all?" I started giggling before I was even done saying it. He cracked a smile, though he tried to hide it. "Thanks for the drinks, Heathcliff. You can head back to the bar. I'm sure the waitress will let you take her home."

Stacey had already walked ahead of us and I began to follow, Heath at my side. "I have no desire to take *her* home. If you weren't so drunk I'd consider taking *you* home."

I knew I hadn't heard him right. "Very funny."

"What's so funny about it?"

Stopping to look at him, he braced me as I wobbled. Slurring my words and scanning his body, I said, "Been there, done that."

Shaking his head at me, he retorted, "I beg to differ. You know you want some of my Heath bar."

Rolling my eyes I retorted, "That should be your hashtag. You can put it on all your dating profiles." He seemed confused and I elaborated. "You know hashtag 'wanna taste my heath bar'. The ladies will eat you up."

Scanning my body, he narrowed his eyes at me. "I'd rather *you* eat me up."

Smacking his chest without thought, I replied, "Too bad I prefer caramel to toffee! And you're a disgusting hedonist." I attempted to wink at him and started walking.

"Ah, big words. Do you even know what it means?"

Stopping once again, I turned and looked up to him. "Don't insult me! Gross, nasty, putrid." He was grinning at me and my quick wit. Without thought, I leaned into him, pulled his head down and then whispered slowly in his ear, "You're the epitome of a hedonist. All about pleasure and all about *you*." Pulling away, I was suddenly filled with desire for him and scrambled away. I caught up to Stacey as she made it to our building, aware he was *still* behind us.

Neither of us objected as he walked into our building with us. Heading to the back stairs, we all proceed up to the second floor as Stacey pulled her keys out of her purse, dropping them. Laughing at her, she eventually ended up on the floor in a fit of drunken giggles. Heath grabbed the keys off the floor and opened her door. I tried to help Stacey up, but ended up on the floor with her. Before I noticed, Stacey was gone and so was Heath. I started wondering if they'd both abandoned me when Heath reappeared in front of me again.

"Where's Stacey?"

"I put her to bed and you're next."

"Wow. That was quick. I think I'll pass if you can't last longer than a few minutes."

Without hesitation and ignoring my remark, he yanked me up and threw me over his shoulder. "Still on the fourth floor?"

"Heathcliff Kerrigan, put me down!" I smacked his back, but it was hopeless.

"When and where Lucille? I can guarantee you that my libido would have you begging me to stop."

"That's doubtful." Groaning at his innuendo I spit out, "Fourth floor, apartment D."

He practically jogged up the flight of stairs to my floor and was still breathing normally when he reached my door. "Key?"

"Pocket." He set me on my feet and I dropped my head against the wall as I fought the dizzy spell trying to take me down.

"Don't hurl on me. I know that look." He started digging in my pockets and I was so focused on not hurling that I didn't even enjoy it. The door clicked open and he escorted me inside.

"You can go. I'll be fine." I ran to the bathroom and hurled in the toilet just in time. A second longer and I would've had a huge mess to clean up.

"Glad I paid for all those drinks for you to just hurl them."

"Go away! Why are you still here?" I took the cold rag he offered, wiping my face with it. "Please, Heath. I'm fine." I was so humiliated. I couldn't stand Heath—at least that's what I told myself—and he was the last person I wanted seeing me that way. I managed to stand and brush my teeth after Heath stepped out.

When I exited the bathroom, he asked, "Have any Motrin or Tylenol?" Nodding, I pointed toward the kitchen and sat down on the couch. He headed to the kitchen and came back with a couple capsules and a glass of water. "Here."

"Thank you."

Sitting down next to me, he wrapped his arm around my shoulders. Without resisting like I should have, I rested my head on his shoulder. If I hadn't been so drunk I would've thought to ask what cologne he was wearing. He smelled so good. I also told myself I only wanted to know so that when I had someone to buy cologne for, I'd know what *not* to buy. His fingers rubbed delicate circles over my exposed shoulder, having an unexpected effect on me.

"Heath?"

"Lucy?" I didn't respond because what was there to say? I wanted to finally be able to put him *and* his brothers behind me, or so I thought. "You shouldn't drink like that. You could've gotten into some serious trouble."

"I'm a big girl, Heath." His hand continued caressing my upper arm and started moving lower, rubbing over the back of my bra. Pulling away, I made the mistake of looking into his eyes.

"Yes, you are." His other hand moved toward my face as his forefinger traced my jawline. "You're not little Lucy anymore. The pigtails are gone and so is..."

He didn't finish his sentence and my eyes moved to his full lips, willing him to speak, or do something, *anything*, with those lips of his. Before I could stop myself, I placed a kiss on the center of his chin, tracing my fingers over the stubble that lingered there.

"Lucy..."

Oh, God. What was I doing? A second before I pulled away, his hands cupped my face and my whole body froze. I'd been here before; in Heath's arms and receiving his kisses. Only, ten years earlier I thought it was his twin brother, William, not Heath, who was adorning me with them. They were identical twins and it had been the last time I mixed them up.

"Heath..."

His lips brushed mine and my body grew limp as my hands searched for something to hold me up. Finding his forearms, I dug my nails into them as his fingers caressed behind my ears. Whimpering, my body needed to get closer to his, but my mind screamed at me to get away from him.

I ended up straddling his lap, my flared skirt easily accommodating, as his hands continued to move over my back. Our teeth gnashed against each other and I felt his lips turn up into a smile against my own. My fingers began working loose the buttons of his shirt and his own hands moved under the back of mine. His hands were so warm and large against the small of my back. He was well-built, always had been, and I loved the feel of his large body under my small one.

My hands worked over his shoulders, kneading and tugging as they went. Pulling my lips away, he sucked on my tongue before letting go, and when he released my swollen tongue, I worked my mouth back to his ear. Leaning back, he let me suck on his neck while his hands traveled over my bare legs. It'd been over a year since I'd had sex and I was horny, but I didn't do one night stands. Not often, anyway. Pushing the moral dilemma aside, again, I leaned back to stare at his face. He was so beautiful and everything I loved to hate. Or was he everything I hated to love? I decided then and there that I was going to have him between my legs that night, begging for more, if it was the last thing I did.

His hands were under my skirt resting on the top of my thighs, playing with the waistband of my panties. Dropping my face to his, I kissed him deeper as he pulled me closer, his crotch pressed into mine. Slowly, I rocked against his erection, willing his clothes away. My hand moved between our bodies as my fingertips dipped underneath his buckle and into his pants. He inhaled, giving my hand more room and I found his silky tip just below the surface.

"Lucy." My name was barely intelligible as he groaned.

I started rocking against him again, in an absolute frenzy of need. "Heath," I whispered, it was building in me quicker than I expected. What the hell? Not this quick. "Oh, shit." Trying to slow it down, I stopped moving.

I squealed when he stood up, my body clinging to his. He pried my legs from around his waist and set my feet on the ground. "Lucy, I can't do this." I pushed back from him, completely separating our bodies, both of us still breathing heavy, and ignored his words, knowing I hadn't heard him right.

I had his pants down and around his ankles before he could fathom what was happening. He wasn't wearing underwear and I smiled in anticipation, on my knees, as his cock stared me in the face. My hands ran up each thigh in unison as my eyes looked to his face. He seemed unsure, but I knew what I wanted. Tenderly, I ran my nails underneath his sack before gripping his base. Swirling my tongue around his head, I was aware of profanities flying from his mouth.

My panties clung to me, soaked with desire and need. A need I hadn't felt in such a long time. I couldn't help but touch myself with my free hand. His hands were in my hair, holding it back as I devoured him. For several minutes I worshipped his cock with my mouth.

He gently rocked his hips, our bodies in sync. "Lucy..." Raising my eyes, but not stopping, I found him staring at me. I'll never forget the look on his face. He was lost and found all at the same time. "Don't look at me that way."

I wasn't sure what he meant and didn't have time to think about it. His balls leapt up and I felt his whole body tense. My hand held on as I took him as deep as I could just in time for him to shoot down my throat. Pulling my other hand from my panties, I released him from my mouth and stroked him with both hands. His body flinched as I stroked every last drop from him.

He sat back down and I seized the opportunity to climb up his body. He was catching his breath when I whispered in his ear, "I'm so close. Make me cum, Heath." I nestled my wet panties against his semi-hard dick and moved against him. He didn't move, except for his heaving chest, so I started nibbling on his neck. Suddenly he pushed me off of him, stood, and pulled his pants back up. "What's wrong?" I hiccupped and smiled, still feeling the effects of the alcohol I'd consumed.

"I can't take advantage of you like this. Not you." I was in shock and didn't know what to say.

But that didn't last long. "Take advantage of me? Screw you. I'm taking advantage of you!" Standing, I threw myself at him and grappled with his belt buckle.

"Lucy. Stop."

"Heath. It's just one night. It's not like I expect anything more from you."

"That's the problem. You're drunk." I dropped my hands as he ran his own over his jaw. "I should've stopped it sooner."

What? I was so confused. Heathcliff Kerrigan—man whore—was not about to turn me down, was he? "What do you mean that's the problem?" Because I just wanted one night or because I was 'drunk'? I wasn't drunk, dammit!

He turned his back, walking toward the door to my apartment. "You're Lucy."

"You're Heath. We've met. Now let's fuck." I was losing my patience and all sense, being more forward than I'd ever been before with anyone.

"Don't you get it? I can't have you like *this*. It's not just *one* night with you."

I'm pretty sure he saw the hurt cross my face as I protested, "Yes, it *is* just one night. That's all I need from you." I'd had a few one night stands with guys over the years, but they were never my idea. Heath knew me better than I thought he did. "I'm not asking you to marry me. And besides, I already had you."

I watched him as he seemed to be debating what to do and what to say next. "You're like my sister, Lucy." The one thing he could say to get me to back off fell from his lips.

The tears immediately pricked at my eyes. "Don't! Don't you say that to me." My chest began constricting. "So, you'll let me suck you off, but you won't return the favor." I waited for him to object and he just stared at me. "See! I was right." I was gasping by then. "You're a fucking hedonist!"

"Lucy…"

He moved to me and I tried to fight him off when he reached for me, but the alcohol and emotions got the best of me. He cradled me to his chest as I began crying, "I hate you, Heathcliff Kerrigan."

"I know. It's better that way." What was he talking about? He lifted me in his arms and sat back down on the couch. "You need to sleep. You won't remember any of this come morning." I prayed he was right. I let myself drift off to sleep, swaddled by the heat of his body.

When I woke, remembering everything, I found myself still on his lap, his head dropped back as he lightly snored. I thought to myself about that summer, ten years ago, when he pulled that prank on me. I thought I was sharing my first kiss with William. Yes, I had been infatuated with William, but he never paid me any attention. Heath, well, he was constantly giving me attention. Attention I didn't want and clearly he had no plan to ever stop. Of course, maybe he got all he ever wanted from me. Ashamed at myself, I tried pushing the memory of me giving him a blow job from my brain.

As he slept, I whispered, "Fool me once, shame on you. Fool me twice, shame on me." Then I climbed off his lap, covered him up with a blanket, and made my way to my room, alone.

I woke up in the morning and headed out of my bedroom, unsure if I'd find him there or not. He wasn't on the couch where I'd left him and there was no note and no sign that he was ever even there. The way it was meant to be.

~ CHAPTER 3 ~

~ LUCY ~

A few days later I received an interesting phone call. One of the matchmakers I'd recently connected with was looking for participants for a new project she was part of. She wouldn't divulge too many details, but I was interested. I mean, it wasn't like I had anything to lose. I wrote down the address and date for the initial information session and interview process that was taking place later that week.

That Thursday evening I sat in a room with a few dozen women as we awaited to hear what this so-called experiment was about. We were informed that professional therapists, matchmakers, and spiritual advisors were looking for candidates who were willing to marry a complete stranger. But that stranger would be matched with you based on personality traits. It would be a lengthy process of questionnaires and interviews to increase the odds of finding your best match. For those willing, we were told the process could be done in a few months, or it could take much longer. They would create a database and wait for a match.

Once all the news was revealed, I looked around to see that more than half the attendees had disappeared. Me, I was intrigued. A group of experts wanted to pick a husband that was a match for me. I was IN! It was crazy and I didn't care. It made complete logical sense to me. Let the interview begin!

Another couple weeks passed. I was still going through the interview process and had stopped checking my dating profiles. I figured it was the right thing to do to commit to the experiment wholly. I was off the market. I had yet to tell my friends and family. I hadn't even told my best friends that I was partaking in the experiment. Stacey had brought it up in conversation last week after hearing about it in the papers and we all joked about the absurdity of it all. Little did they know I had participated and was still going through the process.

Early the next week, Odysseus—though everyone called him O—Heath's youngest brother, was sitting in my hygienist chair. He was a year younger than me, and like his four older brothers, had been given a name his Literature professor mom had picked. It was quite comical, but also spoke to their mother's love of all things literature. Dorian was the oldest, then twins Fitzwilliam and Heathcliff, followed by D'Artagnan and lastly, Odysseus. I loved Mrs. Kerrigan, but some may agree that she was certifiable.

"How are you, O? Long time no see."

"I'm good. Yourself?"

"Good."

I got him all set in my chair, took x-rays, and then got to cleaning. We didn't talk about anything too personal. He was actually home from a recent tour of duty, he didn't elaborate more, but said he was planning to re-enlist.

I was wrapping up his appointment when he said, "Heath asked me to tell you hello."

My heart stopped. "Oh? That's nice."

He chortled, "You two really don't like each other do you?"

"Umm."

"I'm just giving you a hard time. It'll take a special kind of woman to deal with him. Hell, he may have found her."

He was seeing someone? My mind started racing. That had to be why he turned down my advances. Well, after he let me get him off. Fucker. "So, Heath's seeing someone?"

"I think so. He won't spill the beans, but he's clearly love struck or something. We've gone out almost every night since I've been home and he hasn't taken a single girl home."

Sonofabitch! "That's great." I tried to sound happy for him. Heath could take his heath bar and get bent.

"Rumor has it Will's talking about getting married, too." My eyes were probably bugging out of my face. What the hell was he talking about? "Shit. I probably wasn't supposed to say anything, I just figured since our parents are so close."

"He is?"

"It's no biggie, really. Forget I said anything." Before I could ask any more questions, O kissed my cheek and disappeared from the office.

Will and Heath were both off the market. Wasn't that what I wanted? What I needed? Yes. I wanted to put them both behind me. I convinced myself to be happy for them. They both deserved happiness. Well, that might have been stretching it.

That weekend Stacey and Jaime had planned a night out. There were six of us in our group. We'd met at my apartment and then walked to the same bar I'd run into Heath all those weeks earlier.

We were dancing and drinking, enjoying our night of fun when his figure walked through the door. All four brothers were right behind him. This was a rare and amazing sight. All so different, except for Will and Heath, and all amazingly sexy. Will was just as good looking, but more put together than Heath, if that was even possible. Not a single hair was out of place and he was always clean-shaven and wore thin brimmed glasses.

O spotted me and didn't hesitate to come over and join in the fun. Jaime bowed out, her swollen baby belly taking its toll on her. She sat at our table and Dorian followed her and D'Artagnan followed suit, always his oldest brothers shadow.

Will walked over, leaving Heath at the bar talking to the same waitress from weeks back. I accepted Will's hug and moved to a nearby table, needing a break from all the dancing.

"I hear congrats are in order?" He immediately looked annoyed. "Sorry, I wasn't supposed to say anything. O…"

"Of course O opened his mouth."

"He just said that you were off the market. Considering marriage?"

He just grunted and then added, "Something like that."

Narrowing my eyes at him, I asked, "You seem nervous. Cold feet?"

"You could say that. It's a big step."

"So, it's true! Who's the lucky girl?"

"You wouldn't know her." He mumbled something under his breath, but I didn't catch it.

Heath came over and handed Will a drink and just nodded to me. Will left abruptly and went and sat with Dorian, D'Artagnan, and Jaime. Heath and I stood in awkward silence as I focused on the song playing. The song couldn't have been any more inappropriate given the situation. *Me & U* by Cassie was playing and I hoped he wasn't listening to the lyrics.

"You want to dance?"

His words surprised me and I just shook my head in refusal. We stood there for far too long, neither of us speaking. I debated confronting him about the last time I saw him and was about to say something, when Stacey pulled me to the dance floor with her.

We danced for a while and I was beginning to feel like I was on display. I caught Dorian, Heath, and O all staring at me at some point. Was this another brotherly thing? Did I have food between my teeth? Did they know? Had Heath told them what happened? Maybe they were *those* kind of brothers. *Jesus! Get it together Lucy!* I waved a hand to Stacey and headed to the bathroom alone.

I checked myself in the mirror and didn't see anything wrong. Maybe it was time to call it a night. When I left the bathroom, Heath was leaning against the wall. I tried to ignore him and sidle past, but he put his arm up, blocking my path.

"Let me go, Heath."

Instead his other arm came up and he backed me up against the wall, his figure towering over me. "I don't want to let you go."

Now he was fucking with my head. "You had your chance."

"And I blew it. I know. Let me try again."

His breath tickled my forehead as I stared at the open collar of his shirt. I could feel the heat radiating off of him. Turning my face upward, I grabbed his neck and yanked his lips to mine. His hands found my ass and picked me up, anchoring me against the wall behind me. His hips pressed against me as his tongue licked at my mouth.

"Lucy." His voice pulled me from my short lived daydream. "Are you alright?" Before I could respond, he grabbed my hand and pulled me out the back door. Once we were outside, he dragged me down the alley, where we were virtually out of sight. "Let me try again."

"What are you talking about? Try what?"

"You, us..."

Had he lost his mind? "Heath. You're too late. I'm spoken for." I looked up to his face and he appeared dumbstruck. Served him right. I took the opportunity and ducked under his outstretched arm to my escape.

But, I wasn't quick enough.

"It's never too late."

His hands captured my face, digging into the back of my neck as his lips bruised my mouth. Fiercely, my hands gripped onto him as he pushed me back against the brick wall. His body was so heavy against mine, I thought I might disappear into the wall, or into him.

"I want you, Lucy." He sucked my lower lip between his teeth and then ran his nose up along mine. Cinnamon. Was it fireball or gum? He tasted like cinnamon all those years ago, too.

Pulling his mouth back to mine, I pressed my hips into him. His hands traveled down my back, over my ass and one reached down to cup me through my leggings. I moaned, loudly, as he pressed his fingers against me. He could feel every curve and every drop of moisture through the thin fabric.

"I'm not a hedonist. Quite the opposite."

Stuttering, I dared him on. "P, prove it."

His hands moved to the front of my body, one hand gripping my neck and the other working its way into my pants. "How close are you?" I couldn't remove my eyes from his, transfixed by him. "Close as you were that night?"

That night? What night? I couldn't think straight and when I didn't answer his hand ceased moving. I cried out in protest as one side of his mouth curled up at me.

"I, I don't know. Please, make me cum, Heath."

His lips dropped to my neck and whispered in my ear. "Say it again."

"Please."

Biting my neck he demanded, "No, the other part."

His fingers were so close to my sweet spot that I was worried I'd start screaming at him if he didn't stop teasing me. "Make me cum?"

"Again." His fingers roamed over my wet panties. "Were you this wet that night?"

Nodding and turning my neck to give him better access, I arched my back. My arms were flaccid against my body as he held me in place, still gripping my neck. Had it been anyone else, I probably would've been scared, but instead it was fucking hot.

- 36 -

"Yes. Make me cum, Heath."

"I'm gonna make you cum right here, where anyone can see and you're not going to hold back." He looked into my eyes expecting an answer to which I just nodded.

Pulling the fabric aside, his fingers dipped between my soaking lips. "Oh, God."

My head dropped back against the wall as my hands moved to grab hold of him. Finding the front pockets of his pants, I slid my hands inside, finding the side of his erection. I traced my fingers over it and was rewarded with two fingers fucking me. His teeth nipped and sucked on every part of my neck from earlobe to collar bone. The hand that gripped my neck was now under my shirt and pulling the cups of my bra down.

Tweaking my nipple, once it popped free. "Heath, please." His hand moved to my other breast and repeated the action.

"You're holding back. Louder." He was growling in my ear and I wanted him inside me, and not just his fingers.

"Fuck! I want you to fuck me."

His fingers moved in and out of me with great precision, my leggings pushed down my hips. I could feel the brick wall poking at my backside. "I am fucking you."

"You know what I mean." He sneered at me and just shook his head.

"I'm proving a point." Sucking on my lips, I couldn't kiss him back, too lost in the orgasm that was working its way to the surface. "I'm no hedonist. This is about you. Only you."

"Please…"

Soon his thumb joined in the task, circling my clit. Grabbing his other hand, I put it back to my neck and squeezed his hand. He knew what I wanted and held me in place, pressing his body against me.

"Oh, God. Right there. Don't stop."

"Louder!"

He picked up his pace as I continued crying out. Finally, my orgasm took over as I cried out his name. "Heath! Oh, yes, ohhh."

A few minutes later, hell, maybe it was just seconds, he pulled his fingers out of my body. I was still trembling as his eyes penetrated my own. He ran his wet fingers over my lips before placing them in his mouth and sucking them clean. Groaning at the sensuality of it, I pulled his mouth to mine and kissed away the remnants of my orgasm from his lips.

Suddenly, I heard clapping and turned. I was mortified. Will was standing not more than ten feet away, puffing on a cigarette. "That was hot. Well done." Taking a drag, he pulled it out of his mouth and offered it over. "If that doesn't call for a smoke, nothing does."

~ CHAPTER 4 ~

~ LUCY ~

Oh, my God! Had he seen it all? Frantically, I pulled my leggings back up and turned to fix my bra, trying to put myself back together. Heath stood between us, but wasn't saying a word. Why wasn't he telling Will to get the hell out of there?

"Took you long enough. I only handed her to you on a silver platter ten years ago."

What the fuck?

"Fuck you, Will." Finally, Heath spoke.

"Please, we all know I could've had her in my bed ten years ago if I wanted. I did you a solid. I just didn't know you'd take so long to close the deal."

I was shaking I was so angry. Before I knew it, Heath clocked Will across the jaw. I was so embarrassed. I had to get out of there. Running back in the exit we'd walked through a short time earlier, I scurried to our table.

Jaime was heading out and I seized the opening and walked her out to her car that was parked in front of my building. After she pulled away, I ran inside. Dropping back against my door, I closed my eyes and took a deep breath. Just when I figured the coast was clear, my body bounced with the knock that came on the door. Stacey? Please, let it be Stacey.

I opened the door without thought and instead was greeted with his brooding face. "What the hell did you mean you're spoken for?"

This dude was pissing me off and I wasn't about to elaborate. Not now. "Really? That's what you want to talk about? Heath, you need to leave." Making his way inside, I slammed the door in frustration and waited. He turned and we entered a stare off. Neither of us willing to budge or say anything.

After God knows how long, I caved. "Heath. Please. I don't want to do this with you."

"That's not answering my question. Who is he?"

I was growing agitated and old pains were resurfacing. "Didn't you toy with my heart enough that summer? How could I ever trust you?" He took a deep breath and turned away. "And just now. Did you know he was watching? I, I can't do this with you."

I watched him run his hands through his hair before he turned back to me. "What does it matter if he saw? And haven't I paid for my crimes? I was a stupid eighteen year old boy. I didn't expect you to be so hurt."

"Then what did you expect? I was fifteen Heath. You were my first kiss and let me believe you were William the entire time. If O hadn't walked in on us, who knows what else I would've given you."

"You were so infatuated with him. I was jealous."

"Jealous of what? You always treated me like the kid sister you never wanted."

He crossed the room and looked into my eyes. I couldn't bear to look at him, trying to turn away, but he held my face, forcing his eyes upon mine. Slowly, enunciating every word he repeated, "I was a stupid boy, Lucy. Please."

"I…"

"You wrecked my whole world and everything I thought I knew that summer."

"You weren't the only one who was wrecked, Heath." My voice cracked and was barely above a whisper.

"I know I'm not the only one who feels it. The way your body reacted to mine last time I was here and just now in the alley. I know you feel it."

"You mean when you stopped and said I was like a sister and you couldn't do it, do ME?"

"Dammit, Lucy. Stop twisting my words. What about just now, in the alley?"

All I could remember was what his brother had said. I felt like some chew toy they were playing tug of war with.

"You won't remember anything in the morning." I glared at him demanding, "Am I twisting that?"

He pushed himself away from me and paced my floor. "Lucy…"

"Heath, what do you want from me?"

In two long strides, he closed the distance between us and crashed his lips against mine. My body tensed and immediately turned to jello as his arms held me against him. His body was crouched over, accommodating our height difference. God how I wanted to just let him have his way with me, or have my way with him, again, but there was one simple problem. I didn't trust him.

His beard tickled down my neck as he nipped and sucked on my flesh. A tremor coursed through my slight frame and it wasn't missed by him. Growling in approval, his hands kneaded my back before reaching my ass.

I had to stop it. "Heath, please…"

"Please, what?" There was a slight ring of humor in his voice and I knew what I was about to say wasn't what he was expecting.

"Stop. You have to stop."

Leaning up, his eyes searched mine. "Why?"

It broke my heart to say it, but it had to be said. "I don't trust you. We can't do this." He tentatively released me and I backed away from him. I could see the hurt that flashed across his face before it turned to stone.

"I would never…"

Cutting him off I said, "You already have."

"So, that's it? No looking back. No regrets, Lucy? Because I know I have them. I'm trying to fix it!"

That was the problem. We couldn't be fixed. You could only fix something that was broken and we were never broken because we were never really one. I sat on the couch and put the wall up. The tears may have been falling, but I shut down. I could not do this, not with him. There was too much history between us and I didn't know if that hurt our chances or bettered them.

"Once I leave, I'm not coming back." His legs were a blur in my distorted vision. I heard him take a deep breath before he spit out. "Ok. I get it. I thought you were a risk taker. Apparently I was wrong. We're done. I won't bother you again."

I jumped when the door slammed shut behind him. Falling on my side, I curled up on the couch and prayed I'd made the right choice. I was a risk taker. I just wasn't willing to risk my heart on him.

Several months passed and I didn't see or hear from him. I caught myself looking for him at the bar when I was there and never found him. Was it possible that I missed him? He had been a fixture in my life for so long that I attributed my sense of loss to that. The hurt passed and like a minor scrape, it healed. The scar that remained only visible to me.

~ CHAPTER 5 ~

~ LUCY ~

It was a Friday when I got the phone call. This was the event that I was convinced changed the course of my life. Silly me. That event had already happened.

I couldn't believe it! They found a match for me. Forcing myself to take some deep breaths, I sat down on my couch, after I dropped my purse down next to me. I may or may not have fist pumped my hands and stomped my feet on the floor, one after the other. Then the gravity of it hit me. How to tell my family and friends? Errr, maybe it'd be best if I didn't tell them. Shit! Why hadn't I thought about that part? I didn't think there was any chance they'd find my match so I hadn't worried about what I'd tell everyone. Joke was on me!

So *the* joke was now becoming a reality. Why I hadn't run for the hills when the details were spilled was beyond me. The idea intrigued me, maybe it was the hopeless romantic in me. Hours and hours were spent answering questions and filling out forms. I was still convinced that the panelists knew more about me than I did. I never expected to hear back and didn't recognize the number when it flashed across my cell phone.

"Lucy, its Dr. Phillips. Can you stop by my office today after work?"

"Sure. Everything ok?"

"Yes. We just have a few more questions for you."

After work I had made my way to her office and all five panelists were there. Nervously, I sat down as they each asked how I'd been.

"So, what would you say if we told you we found your match?"

I gasped, thinking it was a joke. "What?!"

"We found your match."

They found my match and we were getting married IN THREE WEEKS! They had originally been skeptical given my age and I understood. I'd just recently turned twenty-five and met their age minimum requirement by four days.

I sat and debated who the hell to call first?

"Oh, my God! O.M.G. Holy mother..."

My phone began ringing and it was Stacey, like she could sense me thinking about her in the force. We both had a knack for calling just when we needed one another.

"Hey! I was just thinking about you." I listened to her chatter on and we agreed to meet at the bar down the street for dinner and drinks.

I changed into some jeans and flats before grabbing my purse and headed out the door. Walking past her apartment it all hit me. Crap! Living in the same building as Stacey would most likely change after I was married. I had no idea where my match lived, only knowing we were in the same Metropolitan area. My stomach flipped at the thought. I was getting married and I couldn't imagine my husband would want to live in my dinky apartment.

Stacey was that one friend. You know, *the one* who's against marriage and all things commitment. It was humorous and sad at the same time, considering she was the only one of my friends who'd been married and was already divorced. She'd married her boyfriend of two years in Vegas and they divorced less than a year later, but theirs was a story for another day.

We sat down in our usual booth across from each other. The waitress came right over and took our drink order. We exchanged our typical daily blow by blows. Ha! Wait until she heard what I had to say. The waitress set our drinks down.

She eyed me carefully. "Spill it, ho! You have a secret."

I took a long sip of my drink, through the ridiculously thin straw, and rolled my eyes at her. "You could say that." She was going to flip her lid. "I'm getting married."

She just stared at me like what I'd just said was the most believable thing ever. "Ha, ha. And I'm the next Princess Diana!" When I pursed my lips together, swirling my drink with the ridiculously thin straw, and remained silent, she spoke. "What the FUCK? Are you serious!?"

Shrugging my shoulders, I couldn't contain my giggle when I confirmed it. "Yup. Remember that article you read in the paper?"

"Shut. Your. Face."

"I didn't say anything because I didn't think there was any way in hell I'd get picked."

"Hang on. I need something stronger before I listen to any more."

Stacey flagged down our waitress and ordered a round of shots for us and some chips and guacamole. Once the waitress set down the small glasses, Stacey threw back her shot and asked for another. Oh, boy. It was going to be one of *those* nights. Well, so be it. Once the waitress had replaced the empty shot glass with another, along with our appetizer, we each dug into the chips.

"Ok. So, who is he?"

"Well, that's the thing. I don't know."

"When do you get to meet him?" I just stared at her. "You mean, seriously? I thought that was a joke. You don't get to meet him till that day!" Looking down at the chip in her hand, she mumbled, "I thought I was the crazy one!"

"Stacey!"

"No. It's a good thing. You're sure?"

Shrugging my shoulders, "Is anything ever *for sure?* I've had no luck on the dating sites, you know this, and I've been single for two years. I want…more. I feel like part of me is missing and I don't want to keep waiting for him to find me. I want to find him, too!" She didn't say anything. "Stacey, please say you'll support me in this."

"Bitch. Of course I support you. You're crazy, but I support you. If this works, maybe I'll try it." We both laughed. "So, when's the big day?"

"Saturday, in three weeks." She started choking on her drink as I giggled.

"Do Rick and Rhonda know?" Rick and Rhonda were my parents and I didn't have to say anything for Stacey to know that I hadn't told them. "Want me to come with you?"

"I don't know. They're weird. You know how they are."

She laughed knowingly at my comment. My parents were hell-bent on me marrying one of the Kerrigan boys, but could never agree on one, and I'm sure the thought of an arranged marriage was foreign to even them. Now I was doing just that.

"They're going to be heartbroken that you're not marrying one of the five Kerry boys."

"Kerrigan." I corrected her. This was a constant thing. I don't know if she said their name wrong just to annoy me, but it worked.

Heading to my parents' house the next morning, the nerves filled me as I debated on how I was going to tell them. Flipping through my songs, I turned the speakers up and lost myself in the lyrics. *Believe* by Mumford and Sons is what I decided on. Thoughts of him ran rampant through my head, like an intruder, I begged him to leave.

Part of me wanted to call Heath, though I wasn't even sure if I had his number, and confront him, yet part of me knew it was a lost cause. *I hate him*. That's what I kept telling myself. At least, I wanted to hate him. We could never work.

"Stupid fucking ridiculous childhood crush. That's all it is!" Though I always made myself believe my crush was on Will. And, maybe it was, until *that* summer. The tears began falling and my head started pounding again as I remembered the night in the alley. "Let it go, Lucy. Something even better is waiting for you. You just have to believe."

I made it to my childhood home an hour later, just in time for lunch. Sitting down on the couch, my mom brought sandwiches out for all of us. She made my favorite; turkey and Muenster on a lightly toasted bagel. I took a bite knowing I needed to get some food into me. I was almost done when Dad broke the silence.

"What's going on, kiddo?"

Taking a deep breath I decide to just spill it. "I'm getting married."

~ CHAPTER 6 ~

~ LUCY ~

They took the news a lot better than I thought they would, once they realized I wasn't joking. I explained the whole thing to them and they listened attentively. My older brother was married with kids and I knew they wanted the same thing for me. I made them promise to keep it to themselves. I didn't want the Kerrigan's knowing, only wanting immediate family and my closest friends in attendance. Reluctantly, they agreed.

"So, what happens if on paper you're a match, but in person you're not?"

"We have to agree to give it a good try for two months. After two months we have to decide whether to stay married or to get a divorce."

"Wow."

"I know it's a lot to take in. I trust the panelists and that they have my best interests at heart. It's all about trust, in them and in him; whoever he is."

"More like blind trust."

"You could say that." '

"I just wish we knew something, anything, about him."

"Give me some credit, Dad. I'm picky and the panelists have my mile long list of wants, desires, and dislikes."

"I sure hope so!"

I smiled at my Dad and then asked the inevitable. "Will you give me away?"

Standing up, he embraced me, "Of course. No one else gets that privilege but me."

Heading back to the city, Stacey, Jaime, and I were meeting to go dress shopping. I had no time to waste. I probably should've invited my mom, but I think she needed time to decompress everything. They said they supported me, though it's not what they had planned for me. At least they knew enough to know that their plans for their little girl weren't the same plans I had for myself. It wasn't necessarily what I had planned either, but something about the whole thing felt right, like divine intervention or fate.

A majority of the wedding plans were taken care of for me. I just had to find a dress and be to the church on time. I didn't even know my groom's name and I wouldn't know it until I met him at the altar. I must have been out of my mind. How was it that the panelists didn't have me committed? Maybe they figured marrying me off to a complete stranger was better punishment.

Stacey and Jaime met me at the retail bridal salon and we started pulling dresses off the racks. Jaime was even more supportive than Stacey was. We'd all been friends for a few years, having met in college. Jaime was almost nine months pregnant by then, with her first child. The father, her college sweetheart, Beau, though they weren't married, yet.

"So when is your baby daddy going to put a ring on it?"

"Hell if I know, but he better hurry up."

Stacey and I shared a glance, knowing that Beau already had the ring. What the hell was he waiting for? I found a dress quicker than I thought possible. The three of us shed some tears, Jaime more than me and she blamed the hormones.

"I can't believe you're doing this!"

"I know! I'm so excited and ready for this." Hesitating, I add, "I just hope he likes me."

"Girl, are you crazy? You're smoking hot and you're a keeper. Any man would be lucky to have you. Speaking of, what the hell happened between you and Heath?"

"Heath?! Kerrigan? You hate Heath!"

I glared at Stacey after Jaime's outburst. "Nothing happened and it was MONTHS ago."

"So something did happen?"

"No!"

"You sure about that?"

"YES! He's like a brother to me. Gross!" If Heath could use that excuse then I could too.

Jaime bought what I said with no question as I avoided eye contact with Stacey. "Alright. Time for you two to find a dress." Their heads popped up, what looked like disbelief on their faces. "What? Really? Come on. Who else would I ask to be my bridesmaids?"

After I paid for our dresses, insisting to pay for theirs given the circumstance, Jaime headed home. Stacey offered to pick up dinner and I took the dresses home to my place. We were beyond fortunate that no altering of the dresses was necessary. Even Jaime found one that accommodated her baby belly. I'd be lucky if she didn't go into labor at the wedding.

The next couple of weeks flew by. Almost every evening was filled with either working out, my girlfriends, or my parents. Friday, the week before my ceremony I had a group of girls over at my place for a mini bachelorette party. I was gifted with negligees and naughty items of all variety. Sex toys, lube, condoms, were just some of the basics.

The next day I had my last meeting with my panel of experts. We had been talking for several minutes when Dr. Phillips asked something I wasn't expecting.

"Lucy, what if it turns out to be someone you know?"

I started cracking up at the ridiculous thought and realized Dr. Phillips was serious. "I, wait what?" I looked to each of them. "Are you serious? It's someone I know?"

"You know we can't confirm or deny that. Would you still be open to the possibility if it was?"

I felt myself begin to sweat and became nervous. Honesty, it was the best. "Well, if it's one of my ex-boyfriends I don't think I could. There were reasons we ended our relationships."

They studied me intently and just when I was about to ask another question, Dr. Phillips reassured me, "Lucy, we meet hundreds of people over the course of a lifetime. We really are confident about the match we've selected for you. Obviously you're both from the same metropolitan area, so there's always a small chance that you've crossed paths with him. I hope you're as excited as we are."

Taking a shaky breath, I felt a little more at ease. "You had me scared there. I'm not sure my dad would allow me to marry any of my ex-boyfriends either. So, there's that." I clasped my hands together and said to no one in particular, "I just hope he's as invested in this as I am."

They all smiled back at me. "Your match is a good man. I think you'll agree once you meet him."

"Ugh. You're killing me!"

"Very soon! Enjoy your last few days as a single woman. The next time we meet you'll be married!"

I met Stacey at a jewelry store that night. I wanted to get my future groom a gift and I wasn't sure what to get. We looked at watches, cuff links, tie clips, and rings. I didn't have any idea if he even liked jewelry of any kind. Then gold, white gold, platinum, or tungsten? So many decisions!

"I give up. I need to think about this."

I left empty handed.

After a lot of thought, I went back a few days before the wedding and picked out his gift. Then I headed to the store and picked out a card. Once I was home I sat and stared at the card for far too long before the words came to me. I hoped he'd appreciate my sense of humor and if he didn't, then we were probably doomed.

~ CHAPTER 7 ~

~ LUCY ~

That Friday night I checked into the hotel where I'd be getting married the next day. I got a better night's sleep than I had in several weeks. I felt at ease and at peace. In less than a week I would be on my honeymoon and hopefully, falling in love. Ok. Maybe love was pushing it. I'd take deep like, too.

That night my dreams were filled with my childhood and teen years. But mostly of *that* summer and I hadn't had that dream in so long.

My family, along with the Kerrigans always spent a few weeks together at the Kerrigan's summer cottage. It was the Fourth of July and Will and Heath had just graduated high school. Will was still as dreamy as ever. I hadn't talked to him since Christmas and he was more attentive to me that summer than he ever had been before. We took strolls together to the lake and swam together. If he knew I had a crush on him, he was playing it cool.

That night we planned to watch the fireworks with our families. Right when they started, he took my hand in his and

I was overjoyed. I let him lead me away from where our families had blankets spread out on the beach. Leading me to a copse of trees, he sat down against the trunk of a tree and pulled me down to sit between his legs.

I had never been so close to him before and wasn't sure where or how to sit. Gently, he pulled my back against his chest and told me to relax. He pushed my hair off my neck, sending chills down my spine. I could feel his breath against my ear and a flush began to creep all over my entire body. His fingers drew lazy circles over my arms, causing goosebumps to fly all over my body. He smelled slightly sweaty due to the summer heat, but his cologne was present.

"Lucy?"

"Hmm."

I tilted my head back and met his chocolate brown eyes. I'm pretty sure I stopped breathing. His hand moved over my cheek and down the sensitive skin of my neck, and I couldn't help but close my eyes. His other hand was at my waist and gently squeezed. This was it. William was going to be my first kiss...and my last.

I waited longer than I figured I would and opened my eyes. He was still staring into my eyes and then he asked, "Have you ever been kissed, Lucy?" I just shook my head. "Good. No one's kiss will ever compare to mine." I didn't understand his meaning until it was all over.

My stomach was convulsing like crazy. Every little touch from him was amplified. He leaned in a little closer, our noses practically touching, and I closed my eyes. His breath smelled of cinnamon and just before his lips touched mine, he traced his thumb over my bottom lip, pulling it down slightly.

"Soon they'll be swollen..."

His soft lips met mine and my heart swelled. Cinnamon breath and the smell of William filled me up. Nervously, I reached for his body, not sure where to put my hands. Placing them on his chest, his muscles flexed under my hands. He licked at my lips and I opened my mouth to him. He tasted of cinnamon, too, and I licked back. Shifting closer to me, I felt his hardness at my hip and moved against him.

Panting, he pulled back, "Careful, Lucy."

"Sorry. Did I hurt you?"

Smiling, he said, "No, quite the opposite." The fireworks finale began and he asked, "Come with me?"

We got up and I followed him, knowing I should've told my parents, but not caring anymore. We made it back to the house long before anyone else. He took me to the room he was sharing with some of his brothers and we sat on the bed. It wasn't long before I was laying on the bed next to him. Our arms and legs tangled in one another while we frantically made out.

He fondled my breasts through my shirt and I moaned at the wonderful feelings it sent through my body. He sucked my bottom lip between his teeth and commented on my swollen lips. "Told you they'd be swollen."

Smiling, I turned my face away from him, still embarrassed at what we were doing. "We should stop before everyone gets back."

Groaning, he began kissing my neck. "I don't want to let you go, Lucy."

"So don't, but we have to be careful." He didn't say anything and I knew he was leaving a hickey on my neck. "William…"

His head popped up and he looked confused. He blew out a hard breath, making me nervous and said, "Lucy, I need to tell you something."

Before I could hear what he had to say, O, his younger brother came bursting through the bedroom door and shattered my world.

O took in the scene in front of him and said, "Sorry, Heath. I didn't know."

I felt sick. I scrambled away from whom I thought was Will and glanced between them. Looking to O I demanded, "This is Heath?"

"Lucy…"

O, laughing, responded, "Of course it's Heath. Will has a girlfriend."

Without another word, O left the room, closing the door as I jumped off the bed. Straightening my clothes, I left the *room knowing Heath was right behind me. I ran past my parents who waved, none the wiser to my predicament. Making my way to the tire swing outside in the back yard, I stood there not sure where to go or what to do. I was so hurt. This whole time, days and days, I thought I was spending time with Will. Hell maybe I was, but it had been Heath the whole time tonight.*

    "Lucy, please let me explain."

    I don't know if it was my body's idea of a warning or of helping me to gain closure, but I woke with a smile. I chose to believe it was my body letting go of all the dreams I had as an adolescent. I was an adult, getting married, and it was time to make new dreams and to let go of my childish ones.

    Lying in bed, I rolled over and looked over my wedding dress that was hanging off the closet door. I was getting married. I was getting married? I was getting married! With a smile on my face, I stretched out like a cat under the covers. My mom, Stacey, and Jaime would be there soon and I needed to shower.

    Staring at myself in the mirror, in a robe and my wet hair piled on top of my head, under a towel, I took a deep breath. My stomach growled just as room service knocked on the door. Opening the door, the attendant walked the tray to the table by the window and placed it down. I handed him some cash from my purse before he left.

It was too quiet. Streaming music through my phone, I sat down to eat. *The Words* by Christina Perri was filtering through the room and listening to the lyrics brought tears to my eyes. What the hell was I doing? I wanted the love and passion and romance that every relationship deserved. And I had no way of knowing if I was going to get that with my match. I mean, they knew that those things were important to me, but it was no guarantee that my match would evoke those qualities.

A knock came at my door. Opening the door, I was relieved to see Stacey and Jaime. They took in my appearance and frazzled state and ushered me to sit, each flanking me.

"Honey, what's wrong?"

"I, it's just, here." I replayed the song for them and we sat and listened. "What am I doing?" I was on the verge of hyperventilating as they tried soothing me.

"Lucy, if you don't want to do this, just say the word." Jaime was rubbing my arm and I saw Stacey's reaction to the statement.

"No. Lucy, I know you. You want this and yes, it's not conventional, but it's you. You'll make this work and so will he. I mean, come on! Look at you." I grimaced at her, knowing at that exact moment I was a train wreck. "Ok, don't look at you, but you're amazing, beautiful, funny, kind. I'd do you!" We laughed at that. "He'll treasure you and you'll treasure him. If he doesn't, he'll deal with me."

Jaime chimed back in, "and me!"

"I'm so scared. What if he's fugly?" I tried smiling and their laughter was contagious. "Or horrible in bed or only wants head?"

"Well, if he's got a nice dick then give the man some head!"

Jaime snorted as I laughed in response to Stacey's remark. "Oh, my God! I lived without orgasms for over a year dating Randy. I can't do that again."

Chuckling, Stacey replied, "Well, his name should have warned you. He was a 'Randy' boy and wasn't concerned with your well-being, just getting himself off."

I shook my head at her, smiling. I covered my face with my hands and groaned. "Who does this? I mean, if he's doing this as a means to find a wife..."

There was another knock at the door and Stacey got up to answer it. If it was my mom, she was early. I recognized the secretary from all of my appointments with the panel that interviewed me. Waving her in, I removed my towel and threw it into the bathroom. She handed me a small box and a card.

~ CHAPTER 8 ~

~ LUCY ~

"What's this?" Smiling, she insisted that I open it. Sitting back down, I opened the card. With a shaky breath, my eyes skimmed over the writing. The words were sweet and had me crying all over again.

"Read the damn card!" Jaime was eager to know what it said and so was Stacey.

To my future wife,

Thank you for taking a chance. If you've gotten half the grief I have, I can only imagine how nervous you are. I can't help but think about you walking the same city streets as me, wondering if we've already met. Like ships passing in the night, I've been looking for you and know that you've been looking for me, too. Now I've found you. From this day on I will be your anchor, the one you can always

depend on. If the sea of life gets
rough, know you can turn to me.
I hope you will be the same for
me…
My anchor.

I can't wait to begin this new
journey with YOU.

~ See you at the altar…
Your future husband

Jaime sniffled, "Oh, God. He's so sweet." I was crying and Stacey was on the verge.

I opened the small box that accompanied the card and opened it up. Gasping, I pulled out a necklace with a silver anchor charm. "It's beautiful." We were looking it over when the receptionist went to leave. "Wait! I have a gift for him, too."

I got up and walked to the dresser. Placing the box and the card in her hands, I said, "Make sure he gets this." She nodded and left.

Stacey asked, "What'd you get him?"

"I guess you'll have to wait and see."

"Alright. So, you're good? Cuz I'm ready to celebrate!"

"Yes, I'm good."

"Alright. Turn that depressing shit off. I have a song of my own I want you to hear."

I turned my music off as Stacey started hers. The song had us cracking up as we listened to it a few times. *Dear Future Husband* by Meghan Trainor put us all in great spirits as we started doing my hair and makeup.

Sitting in the chair a couple hours later, we made the final touches to my hair and makeup. "Ok. I think you're ready. Just need to get you in your dress."

My mom had arrived by then and was sniffling. "Mom, please."

"It's just...I knew this day would always come, but I don't think you're ever ready for it."

"Please! You've been ready to marry me off since I could talk back." We were all laughing.

My mom replied, "Well, yes, that is true. You still have that sass that drove me crazy. Now you get to drive someone else crazy!"

"Yeah. Good luck to the lucky sir." I glared at Stacey and stuck my tongue out at her.

"Don't mess up your makeup!"

"Yeah, yeah."

We pulled my dress off the hanger and began the tedious process of lacing up the corset back. Once it was on, I had Jaime put the anchor necklace around my neck. I stood back and looked in the mirror. It was real. I loved the dress. I knew what I'd wanted and was so happy that it actually looked good when I'd tried it on at the store a couple weeks prior.

I hadn't heard my dad walk in and turned to see him. "You're a vision." Smiling, he leaned in and kissed my cheek.

"Thank you."

"So, you're really doing this?"

Touching the necklace that rested above my heart, I replied, "Yes. I'm really doing this."

Nodding, "Ok. They're waiting."

"Ok. I just have to make sure I have everything."

We all did another once-over of the room and put my bags by the door. They'd be moving my belongings to the honeymoon suite once the wedding had taken place.

Honeymoon. I had to pack for that, too. All I knew was that we were going somewhere warm. I couldn't wait to get my bikini on and sink my feet into the sand, assuming there would be sand.

My dad and I waited for the next elevator and sent my mom, Stacey, and Jaime on down ahead of us. I knew he just wanted a moment alone with me and I was going to give it to him.

Pulling me close, he whispered, "I love you, munchkin."

"I love you, Dad."

"So, what are you going to do if he's the ugliest man you've ever seen?"

I balked at him. "Dad! You're not helping. I mean, looks are nice, but they're not everything."

"You're asking a lot of me. Giving you away is one thing, but to a complete stranger..." I watched as he pulled at the collar of his shirt. "Maybe we should agree on a word or signal. You say it and we'll high-tail it out of there."

Laughing, I agreed. The elevator doors opened and we stepped inside. "I'll ask for a piece of gum. That work?"

"Got it. One mention of gum and I'll pull my gun and send him running for the hills."

When the elevator doors opened, we were escorted to a private room and told it would be just a few minutes. My mother had been asked to take her seat while Jaime, Stacey, my dad, and I waited. Our bouquets were waiting for us and it seemed like an eternity as we waited. My hands were sweating and my heart was racing.

The room doors opened, "It's time." Jaime and Stacey flashed me their cheesy grins in unison as we headed toward the small chapel the hotel had on site. Standing to the side so that I couldn't sneak a look at my groom, I watched as Jaime and Stacey disappeared into the chapel.

The murmur of voices carried through to where my father and I stood. Almost more than I would expect from people awaiting a bride. I wasn't quite sure what to make of it all. My dad seemed to sense my concern.

"Say the word." I just shook my head.

"I'm sure they're all nervous for us."

The song I had selected to walk down the aisle to, began to play. I wanted something different and chose *History In The Making* by Darius Rucker. The doors reopened and everyone standing blocked my view of my groom. My eyes drifted to the floor and then to my friends and family on my side of the aisle. The nerves were coursing fiercely through me and I was petrified to look at my groom or anyone on his side of the aisle. Finding my mother's eyes, I expected to see her sad and instead she was ecstatic. Apparently I had been right. She was ready to be rid of me.

My father took in a sharp breath and mumbled something under his breath. Darting my eyes to my groom, I froze in my tracks. What the ever living fuck?

"Lucy, what's going on?"

I couldn't breathe and I wanted to blame my tight dress, but knew the dress wasn't that tight and had nothing to do with what I was experiencing. I looked to my mother and then over to the other side of the aisle. His family was just as excited as mine was. Was this a joke?

"Lucy." My father was trying to get my attention and tugged on my arm. "Lucy, is this a prank?"

Shaking my head, I looked to my dad. "I, I don't know." This had to be a joke. There was no other explanation.

I heard him say my name and looked to see him approaching my father and me. "Lucy."

Unlinking arms with my father, I took a step back and put my hand up. "Stop right there." He did just that, the smile leaving his clean-shaven face. "What the FUCK is going on?"

"Lucille Rose!" My mother chastised me, causing him to smirk at me.

"Wipe that fucking grin off your face!" I totally forgot about the guests we both had in attendance and unleashed my fury at him. "You did this didn't you? This is some sick prank. How much did it cost you? Is your brother in on this too?" I glanced to his side and they were all there, minus O who was on another tour of duty.

"Lucy, I swear I didn't know."

"You're a liar!" I was beginning to hyperventilate and I wanted to hurt someone, anything. "You expect me to believe that line of bullshit?" He took another step closer. "Don't you come near me Heathcliff Kerrigan!"

~ CHAPTER 9 ~

~ LUCY ~

Turning, I ran out of the chapel and down a back hall, aware of him and my father calling after me. Finding an empty conference room, I dropped my bouquet on the table and tried catching my breath. That summer invaded my memories once again, specifically that night as I fled his room after finding out *he* was Heath and not Will.

"Explain what? You lied to me. Was it you all week?" I was shaking with the anger and sadness that coursed through me.

It was then I picked up on the mannerisms of Heath and how they were different than William's. His hair was disheveled—always—and he flexed his neck until it popped and his lips pursed. Now that I thought about it, I never saw these actions out of William.

"It's been me the past few days." He moved a step closer and I put my hands up, warding him off.

"Was this all a game to you? I don't understand." I turned my back to him, not wanting him to see any more of my tears.

"Lucy, I, shit. I don't know why I did it."

His hands touched my shoulders and I pulled away just as quick. I turned to see Will and who must've been his girlfriend walking over. She was a skank, I just knew it and I was totally jealous. They were oblivious to my predicament, or were they?

"Aww, lovers quarrel?"

"Shut up, Will."

I heard Will's girlfriend ask how old I was and that just fueled my fire. "Old enough to know that Will deserves better than the likes of you!"

She made a step toward me and I didn't flinch, but Heath stepped between us as if I needed his protection. Will grabbed her hand and they wandered off before anything else could be said between her and me.

"You might want to put a leash on her, Heath." Will's words just infuriated me more.

Turning back to face me, he chastised me. "What's wrong with you?"

Shoving his chest as hard as I could, I screamed, "YOU!"

"Lucy…"

"Stop saying my name. You, you…" I couldn't even finish my train of thought. I was beyond angry. "I need to go."

Stepping in front of me he pleaded, "We need to talk about this, us."

Scrunching my face up I screeched at him, "There is no US, therefore there's nothing to talk about." Motioning my hand between us I bit out, "This never happened. And you and your brother will NEVER fool me again."

He let me pass and I retreated to my bedroom. I had the smallest room in the house, but I was also the only one who had my own room. The perks of being the only girl in both families.

I cried myself to sleep that night and wasn't sure if it was because I knew Will was taken or because I felt like I'd betrayed them both. It was ridiculous to feel like I was the one who betrayed them. They betrayed me, not the other way around. The gravity of finding out that the whole time I thought Will was falling for me, I was actually with Heath. Was Heath really falling for me like he said or was it all part of the scam? I didn't want to know. All I knew was that I detested Heath and the events of that week just solidified it.

Seeing him over the years wasn't something I could get out of. Our parents were best friends. I always put on a happy face and avoided Will and Heath like the plague. I also may have flaunted any boyfriend I had in front of them.

The door flung open, pulling me back to reality. FUCK. How had I let him do this to me again? Had it even been Heath? He was clean shaven and that was typically William's look. Shit! Turning, I saw that it was Stacey, not who I was expecting, but someone I preferred.

"Lucy, what's going on? When I walked down the aisle I was shocked. I thought maybe the two of you had this planned all along."

"I didn't PLAN THIS." Pacing the floor and wringing my hands together I began rambling. "How, why, I don't understand. What did I ever do to him to deserve this?"

Stacey walked over and tried consoling me with a hug, but sat down when I refused her. "Lucy, before you walked down the aisle he was radiating joy. I know I don't know him that well, but I don't think he planned this. Your mom and his mom were talking across the aisle, both so happy and surprised."

Scoffing, "Of course our mothers are happy. They've wanted me married to one of the boys since before my conception." Stacey chuckled and I glared at her.

"Lucy, can I ask you something?"

"Of course."

She took a deep breath, then asked, "What happened between the two of you all those months ago?"

I spit out, "Nothing," before she was finished asking.

"Umm, bullshit."

"Excuse me?"

"Lucy, I've known you long enough to know that something happened. You know I don't care, just tell me. Maybe it'll help."

Turning away from her I found a chair and sat in it. Looking out the window I started talking. She knew I disliked Heath, but didn't know about that summer I turned sixteen, and I wasn't going to tell her now. "That night he walked us home we almost ended up in bed together." I left it at that. No one needed to know that I let him blow his load in my mouth like a five dollar hooker.

"Almost? I thought for sure…"

"No. He said I was like a sister to him and then we fell asleep on the couch together."

"Wait, you're like a sister to him, but he stayed the night? I'm confused."

"How the fuck do you think I felt?"

"Jesus. So nothing else happened after that?"

Groaning, I confessed, "The night we were at the bar and him and all his brothers showed up…"

"Yes, I remember. You left with Jaime."

"Yes because we almost did it again in the alley, then Will saw, and I left and he showed up on my doorstep, begging me for a second chance."

"Will saw! Saw what?" Stacey looked as confused as I felt. "Second chance at what?"

Ignoring her first question, I answered the second. "We kind of had a thing when we were teenagers. It's complicated."

She jumped up out of her chair, "I knew it!"

"What the fuck do you mean you 'knew it'?"

"Everyone knows you dislike each other, but it's more than that. You two have like unrequited love for one another or some shit."

"Uh, or some shit. Believe me, there's nothing unrequited about it."

Gasping, she proclaimed, "You're in love with him!"

"'Da fuck? I am NOT!"

Jaime walked in and added, "I think thou doth protest too much."

I wasn't sure how long she'd been standing there, but clearly long enough. "Shut up."

She smiled at me and sat down next to me. "Lucy, he didn't know. He's outside and wants to talk to you. He told me he had no idea. I believe him."

"He who? I'm not even sure if it was Will or Heath."

"Who do you want it to be? What does your gut tell you?"

"Heath. It was Heath." They smiled and nodded. "But, he can't be my match. We hate each other."

They both said it in unison and giggled, "There's a thin line between love and hate."

"Fuck off!"

"Lucy?" All our eyes whipped to the door where Heath stood. "Can I talk to you? Please?" His voice was low and I hated how my body reacted to it, to him.

Without saying two words to me, Stacey and Jaime left the room. Traitors. I turned my chair slightly, resting my elbows on the table. My head was pounding and I began massaging my temples. I heard the leather of the chair exhale as he sat down in the chair closest to me.

"Lucy," I moved my eyes to his and waited for him to speak. "The experiment brought us both here. I promise."

"I don't believe you." My voice cracked and the tears pinpricked my eyes. How could he do this to me? "How could you do this to me?"

Pulling my hands from my temples, he wrapped his large hands around mine. "When I saw you walking down the aisle, I couldn't have been happier. To have you as my wife... I can't explain to you how happy that makes me."

Searching his eyes, I knew in my heart he was telling the truth, but I couldn't wrap my emotions around it all. I couldn't marry him. "Heath, I can't marry you."

His head jerked back slightly, but he never let go of my hands. "Why not?" I didn't have a response and he asked another question. "You're here because the experiment revealed your match, right? How could I have anything to do with that?"

"It's more complicated than that."

"No it's not. It's the best surprise."

"What do you mean? You hate me and the feeling is mutual. I'm like a sister to you. It's bordering on incest."

Chuckling, he asked, "You really think that's how I feel about you?"

Sighing, "Think? You said it yourself all those months ago."

"Lucy, you were drunk. I wasn't going to have you that way, but you were so determined to make it happen. Like a douchebag I let you get me off then I freaked. I said the only thing I thought would get you to stop."

"You're an idiot."

"Yes, we all know this. And your sass is probably going to kill me." I tried holding back the smile as I shook my head at him. "But I'd die happy." I rolled my eyes at him. "When you turned me down, told me you were spoken for... Wait, so was that all a ruse?"

"I'd just applied for the program. I didn't think it would be fair to start something with you when I'd already committed." Prying a hand away, I wiped the drying tears that lingered under my eyes.

"Here." He handed me the decorative handkerchief from his lapel and I spotted the cuff links I'd purchased, solidifying it even more for me.

"Cuff links." I couldn't muster anything else.

"'Stay calm and say I do'. Really, Lucy?" I just shrugged my shoulders. After I handed his handkerchief back to him he said, "Perfect." His fingers moved to hold the anchor hanging from my neck. "I meant what I said in that card." We sat in silence for a minute or two when he said, "So, let's do this."

I snorted and narrowed my eyes at him. "You're out of your mind."

"If I'm out of my mind then so are you. I've known you my whole life."

"Exactly! Hold up. So, when did you apply to the program?" He started to talk and then I stopped him, "Wait, I don't think I want to know."

"Lucy, you don't get it."

"Get what?"

Taking my hands in his again, he confided in me, "I've wanted you since that summer. Don't you know that by now?"

The tears started again. "You had a funny way of showing it. You've had ten years to come and get me. Why didn't you come and get me?"

"Lucy," he moved closer, knees flanking mine, and pulled me to his chest. I let him hold me as he whispered, "Please have faith. They paired us together for a reason."

"More as a joke. All we do is fight. And you gave up on us. You could be marrying a stranger right now."

Sighing, "I never gave up. I just, you're like the unattainable dream." I tried to say something and he shushed me. "As to the fighting…" he sighed, "…silly Lucy. I fight with you because I can't seem to reach you any other way. There's no one else I'd rather fight with."

I asked what I'd wanted to know for ten years. "What really happened that summer?"

"What didn't happen that summer? I fell in love with the one girl I didn't want to fall in love with." I stiffened at his words and pulled back. As if he knew I doubted his confession, he said it again. "I fell in love with you that summer, Lucy. And then like a dumbass I let you walk away from me."

"After you broke my heart."

"I didn't think you cared."

"Me either."

He nodded, "I know. I should've told you it was me from the beginning. But would you have given me a chance? You were so consumed with Will…" He didn't finish. "He's the one who sees you as a sister, not me."

"I, I don't know. We'll never know. We can't know."

"Don't you know? We can know."

"I looked for you, every week, at the bar. You were never there anymore."

"I knew you'd be there. I couldn't handle the risk of seeing you there with *him*. Now I know that *he* never really existed."

He stroked my face with his hands and I closed my eyes. His scent was swarming around me and then his lips were on mine. Gripping his lapels, all I could smell was his cinnamon breath and I licked at the seam of his mouth. Groaning, he tried getting closer to me, but my dress made it almost impossible. Hands circled around me, grasping my bare shoulders. His fingers gently moved back and forth as goosebumps formed on my body.

Heath pulled us to our feet, the height difference became more evident. His erection pressed into my belly as I let my tongue glide over his. I couldn't deny my body's reaction to him. I wanted him. It was purely physical. My hand moved to his face, moving over his recently shaved jawline.

"You shaved. Why?"

Smiling at me, he kissed my nose and said, "I don't know. I haven't kept a beard since that night in the alley. You like it?"

Shaking my head, I said, "No, I prefer the scruff."

"Noted."

He started kissing along my jaw and down my neck. I couldn't hold back the moan that escaped my lips. "Heath." Without thought, my hand traveled to his pants and his cock.

Palming him through the suit pants, he pulsed in my hand and dropped his head to my shoulder, biting down gently.

"Lucy."

"Sorry to interrupt."

I jumped out of his arms and turned to see my father standing there. "Jesus Christ."

My dad was embarrassed, but played it cool. "Should I tell them the wedding is still on? People are asking."

Shaking my head, I started to talk when Heath interjected. "We just need a couple more minutes."

My dad smiled at us both and left the room. Turning back to Heath, "We can't."

"We can!"

"No, we can't."

"Why?"

"I don't know if I can trust you." There it was. That word again. Trust.

Pulling me close and dropping his forehead against mine, he pleaded. "I need you to trust me. Fate keeps throwing you in my path for a reason. We're supposed to be together. I feel it in the deepest parts of me. Let me make this right."

"Heath, I..." His brown eyes searched my blue ones. "I'm scared."

"I'm scared, too. Please, trust me. I'll never hurt you again, Lucy." He dropped down on one knee in front of me and took my left hand in his. "I want you. I want us. Lucy, marry me."

I had entered into this experiment planning to marry my match, who was supposed to be a total stranger. Heath was anything but. But he was my match? I had to stay true to myself, but could I really continue with this experiment and pray for the best?

Conflicting emotions made my stomach churn. I didn't know what to do. My head and heart were both so confused. But I knew I had to say something, had to do something. Stroking his cheek, I was ready to give him my answer. I had to be able to trust more than just him; I had to learn to trust myself.

HONOR

~ PROLOGUE ~

~ HEATH ~

Lucy Roberts.

I had to let her go for good. It was the only thing I knew how to do. I'd done nothing but let her go for the last ten years. Of course she had a habit of walking back into my life when I least expected her. That summer ten years ago when she walked into my family vacation home, no longer a girl, but a young woman, she didn't see me staring at her from the shadows, too immersed in my twin brother's world to notice me. I played the cruelest joke on her that week, not realizing the consequences that would come in the aftermath of revealing my true identity to her. I still wasn't sure why I did it; desperate for her attention or was I trying to pay her back for ignoring me?

Two years after that summer, she shook the ground I walked on once again. She was a high school graduate, headed to the state university. Anytime I tried to talk to her during that week she shut me down before I could even begin. Her actions, or lack thereof, sent me down a dark path that I was ashamed to recall. William was my saving grace then and the only person who could get through to me. He was also the only person who knew what, *who*, my problem was.

Then this past summer when I saw her again— something that happened on occasion considering we lived in the same town—we frequented the same bars, the air between us had changed. I will never confirm or deny that I knew her routine better than she did. If I wanted to find her, I had my ways. That night she was sitting with Stacey, eating, drinking, and laughing. The possessiveness that swept over me that night startled me. It was something I'd buried long ago, or so I thought.

What transpired between us that night was a travesty. I did and said everything wrong and it didn't help that she was drunk and defensive, like she usually was with me. Matters grew worse when I allowed my dick to do the thinking. In a moment of weakness, I let her give me a blow job. It wasn't my finest moment, but fuck, it was *fine*. More arguing and misconceptions left me reeling for weeks.

O, my younger brother, was my distraction during those couple weeks. He was home on R & R and we spent most of our free time together. He joked and teased me and my lack of man-whore tendencies. I wasn't one to hesitate showing a woman a good time. But after that night with Lucy in her apartment, I couldn't fathom being with anyone else. My cock wanted her. My body wanted her. Hell, my soul wanted her.

A couple nights before O was set to leave again, all five of us brothers headed out. I led the way and suggested the bar, knowing where she would be. I blamed Will for the disaster that night turned into. He'd walked up on us, after I'd finger-fucked her in the alley, and made crude remarks. It ended with Lucy running away and me sucker-punching my twin.

"What the fuck is wrong with you?" He was rubbing his jaw and smirking at me.

"If she hates me, then maybe you have a chance."

I shook my head at him. He was trying to help, but was about as useless as I was. "You're a dick."

"Well, are you going to go after her?"

I had looked around to realize Lucy had fled and I was none the wiser. FUCK! I ran after her, but when I found her at her apartment down the street, it was too late. Her wall was up and it wasn't coming down.

I said something to the effect that if she let me go, it was over, we were over. She let me leave without a single objection. She was more trouble than she was worth. That's what I told myself anyway. I spent the rest of that weekend in a drunken stupor. Another mess for Will to clean up and he did. I locked my memories of Lucy away in a box, never to open again. I was a man of my word. It was over, we were over, and it was time to move on.

If you're wondering what made me decide to marry a stranger, it was my twin, Will. He mentioned that he was partaking in this crazy matchmaking scheme and I was intrigued. After the incident with Lucy in the alley that summer night, when everything went to shit, I decided to pursue love. And pursuing it blindly seemed like the way to go.

I began the process of lengthy interviews and waited to see if they could find my match. I wanted to share my life with someone, maybe have a family. A couple months later, sooner than Will or I expected, Will got the call. They found his match. And so I continued my wait.

~ CHAPTER 10 ~

~ HEATH ~

Now it was *my* wedding day. Was I ready for this? Yes! I knew it was time. Looking to my family, O the only one not in attendance, everyone but Will smiled back. He never wanted Lucy so I'm not sure what his problem was.

Lucy.

When she finally spotted me, she freaked as I anticipated she would. I ran after her once her father finished questioning me. I knew she was in the conference room with Stacey and Jaime and I tried being patient. I thought about the letter she'd written me, unaware that I was her groom.

Dear Husband to be,

I'm excited to start this crazy journey with you. I'm scared and hope you'll be patient with me. I'm witty, a little quirky, but very loving. Thank you for taking a chance. And when all else fails, remain calm and set your eyes on me. I hope to always be your home, a place of comfort, rest, and love.

Your future wife.

It was a beautiful letter and so her. Her wit and quirks were what I loved most about her. I had opened the small box that accompanied the letter and found cufflinks inside. They were black, but said 'Stay calm' on one and 'Say I do' on the other. Chuckling, I placed them in my shirt and tucked the card into my breast pocket.

When I heard the girls' voices growing heated, I couldn't take it anymore. Opening the door, I made my presence known and Stacey and Jaime left. Lucy and I laughed, talked, yelled, kissed, all while trying to meet on middle ground.

Pleading with her, feeling vulnerable, but knowing she had to know, "I need you to trust me. Fate keeps throwing you in my path for a reason. We're supposed to be together. I feel it in the deepest parts of me. Let me make this right."

"Heath, I..." I waited, looking into her face, mesmerized by her eyes. "I'm scared."

"I'm scared, too. Please, trust me. I'll never hurt you again, Lucy." The only thing left to do was to officially propose to her and so down on my knee I went. "I want you. I want us. Lucy, marry me."

She hesitated as she stroked my cheek. I said a silent prayer for her to say yes. I'd do anything just to make her mine.

"Now that you know it's me, you're sure you still want me?"

My heart leapt and my stomach jerked. "Lucy, I've wanted you for ten years, maybe longer."

"But why didn't you fight for me?"

Closing my eyes and shaking my head I confided in her. "I'm a stubborn fucking idiot. You should know that by now." Searching her eyes, "I won't stop fighting for us. You have my word."

Her eyes searched my face before she nodded. Her voice cracking, she surrendered, "I want you, too. Maybe just as long."

I knew I was grinning like a fool as I clutched her left hand in mine. "Is that a yes?"

Smiling, "Yes. I'll marry you Heathcliff Kerrigan."

Bounding to my feet, I wrapped my arms around her slight frame, picking her off the ground as we buried our heads in the neck of the other. "Lucy," pulling back to look at her, "you're sure?" I couldn't risk her breaking my heart one more time.

She smacked my arm, "I said yes didn't I?"

That sarcastic tone and smile that I loved was there and I cupped her face. Leaning in I whispered, "Things are never going to be the same." I felt her stiffen as desire swept through her. I knew her well enough to recognize it. Holding her breath, I leaned in and kissed her.

Slowly, our mouths danced to a new tune. She was my fiancee and in a few minutes she'd be my wife. We both knew it. Her tongue searched for mine as I parted my lips, granting her access. The silky warmth caressed over mine as her minty breath mingled with my cinnamon breath.

"I hate to break up your tryst, but everyone's waiting for an answer." It was Mr. Roberts asking what I already knew.

Breaking the kiss I stared into her eyes and gave him his answer without looking at him. "We're getting married." Smiling, I kissed her nose as a blush crept up her cheeks.

"Lucy?"

Peeking over my shoulder she confirmed, "It's ok, Daddy."

"You're sure?"

"Yes. I've never wanted anything more." She smiled at me and kissed the stubble already appearing on my chin.

Was this what love felt like? My chest constricted at her words and I didn't know whether to shout for joy or run for the hills.

"Heath?" Turning to Mr. Roberts, I found his hand outstretched. "Welcome to the family, though you've always been a part of it." Looking to us both he chortled, "Your mothers will both be over the moon." Winking, he left the room announcing, "We're having a wedding. Get your butts back in your seats."

~ CHAPTER 11 ~

~ HEATH ~

Now I stood and waited. Her brother was eyeing me suspiciously and I tried ignoring it. Our mothers were practically cheering in their seats as Will, Dorian, and D'Artagnan were whispering to one another. Crude comments no doubt.

History In The Making by Darius Rucker was playing again and I waited for my bride, my Lucy, to appear. Stacey and Jaime made their way down the aisle and then the doors reopened for Lucy and her father. This time I really took in the sight of her. The dress fit her like a glove, accentuating all her curves. The light sparkled off the dress; lace and sequins flattering one another. The sight of the anchor necklace around her neck had me touching my cuff links in response.

The next few minutes passed like a fog. Before I knew it the Justice of the Peace was having us recite our vows.

"Lucy, place the ring on his finger." She took my left hand in hers and slid the silver band on my finger. "With this ring, I thee wed."

"With this ring, I thee wed."

"Heath, now your turn."

Sliding the ring on her finger I announced, "With this ring, I thee wed."

The Justice was about to start our vows when I interrupted him. "I'd like to say something." He nodded and Lucy looked petrified. I took a deep breath and squeezed her hands in mine. I stared at her for longer than I anticipated when she brought me back to the present.

"Heath?"

"Sorry." A light chuckle filled the room. "I know that things haven't always been easy between us. I meant what I said in that letter. I'm your anchor, your support, your standing stone. I'll always be here for you when you need me. Your wit and humor hooked me long ago and no one has ever been able to make me smile like you do. I know I haven't always been good at telling you that. I look forward to spending the rest of my years honoring you, cherishing you, and trusting you and the leap of faith you're taking today. There's nobody else for me. I know that now." A tear rolled down her cheek—not my intent—but I knew my words had resonated with her.

"Heath…how am I supposed to compete with that?"

Smirking, I replied, "You can't!" Laughter filled the room again and I whispered, "Just stay calm and say I do."

She chuckled and shook her head at me. "I'm speechless."

"Well, that's a first." Smacking my arm, I rubbed the spot and winked at her.

"Ok. Lucy, repeat after me." After we exchanged our traditional vows, he proclaimed, "I now pronounce you Mr. and Mrs. Heath and Lucy Kerrigan. You may kiss your bride."

Pulling her close I whispered so only she could hear. "Our last *first* kiss as husband and wife. Make it count!"

Grinning, she cupped my face as my hands wrapped around the small of her back. She pulled my mouth to hers and we didn't stop until the whooping and cheering turned into groans and moans. She wiped her lipstick from my lips and twining our fingers together, we walked up the aisle, together.

We only managed to get a few moments alone before we were swept into greeting our guests and taking pictures. Everyone had a hard time believing that neither of us knew who we were marrying that day. Lucy seemed nervous, but she also had a look plastered on her face every time she glanced at me, like she had a secret. She wasn't alone.

I wrapped my arm around her back and whispered in her temple, questioning her. "What's going through that mind of yours Lucy Kerrigan? Is it my Heath bar? Can't wait can you?"

She elbowed me and responded, "I told you, I prefer caramel."

"If memory serves, I'd disagree with that. You were quite the fan that night."

She looked up at me with murder in her eyes as I smirked at her. "Shut your mouth. I was drunk."

"Well in that case, let me get you another drink." She huffed out a breath and tried pulling away. "Hey, hey. I'm just messing with you. I'm sorry." Rubbing her upper arms while trying to make eye contact, I bent at the knees to look in her eyes. "Lucy, what's wrong?" Biting her lip—she was nervous—though she was trying to hide it. "You can tell me."

"It's just, we're married now and well…" What was she worried about? "I, we," she looked in my eyes, then to my mouth, "it's expected that we'll consummate things."

I wasn't sure if she wasn't attracted to me—no, I knew that wasn't the problem. "Lucy, we can take it slow." I was about to say something more when she started shaking her head at me and giggling. "What?"

Leaning up to my ear she chimed, "I don't want to take it slow. We've played this cat and mouse game for far too long."

My cock sprang to attention at her confession. As she pulled away I yanked her back to me, our lips a breath apart. "I couldn't agree more." I kissed her slowly and she let me lead it.

I was aware of someone clearing his throat, causing me to pull my lips off hers. Looking to the DJ, he said, "The first dance is in a few minutes. Any requests? I had something picked, but given the situation I wanted to ask if you had a special song you'd rather hear."

Nodding, I looked to Lucy and she just shook her head. She may not remember, but I did. Closing the distance between the DJ and I, I asked for the song I wanted and he confirmed he had it. Maybe hearing it, she'd remember.

"What'd you tell him?"

Kissing her cheek, "You'll just have to wait and find out." Her lip turned up in a smile as I dragged her around the room. "We're being rude to our guests. Come on Mrs. Kerrigan."

We were talking to Jaime and Beau when Jaime excused herself. Lucy started harassing him about when he was going to pop the question. I wasn't familiar with their relationship, but clearly Lucy was.

"Beau, you've had the ring for months and she's ready to pop. What are you waiting for?"

"Actually, I have the ring with me. But I don't want to steal your thunder." Lucy practically jumped out of her skin with excitement.

"Steal my thunder! It's the only thing she wants, Beau!"

He took a deep breath and I felt for the guy. I could only imagine what he was going through. Before we could chat anymore, the DJ came overhead and asked us to the dance floor.

The monotone piano beat started as I took her hand, leading her to the center of the dance floor. Our family and friends all circled around the edge of the dance floor and gazed on as I took my bride in my arms. But would she remember?

I knew the minute she felt it, remembered it. "Heath!"

"I'm glad you remember. Now shut up and let me dance with my wife."

The Reason by Hoobastank played through the room. That song was playing that Fourth of July night in my room while we laid on my bed and whenever I heard it, I thought of her. I had even made a mixed CD or two for her that I never gave her and the song was on all of them. Thinking about how things could've been different had I fought for her all those years ago made me hold her tighter. I also knew that had I fought for her then, I may have not been here with her now.

I heard her whisper my name and when I locked eyes with her, she raised her lips to mine. No longer caring who saw because this amazing woman was now my wife. Mine. We kissed and held each other as the song played on. When the song was almost over, we both had tears in our eyes. Wiping the tears from under her eyes, she tried to smile.

"I forgot that song was on that night." She paused and stroked the back of my neck. "I never knew you were so romantic Heathcliff."

"Shhh." Smirking, I added, "Don't tell anyone."

"Our secret."

As the song ended, the room filled with applause. She took an exaggerated bow and beamed with radiance. We went through the traditional dances, cut the cake, garter and bouquet toss, and things were winding down when Beau started talking on the mic.

Lucy was curled into my side as we listened to Beau pledge his love to Jaime. Then, like something out of a bad comedic romance movie, Jaime peed herself. Lucy quickly corrected me as her, Stacey, and every other woman present fluttered around Jaime. Her water had broken and I knew my wedding night had just gone to shit.

~ CHAPTER 12 ~

~ HEATH ~

It was mid-morning of the next day when we got back to the hotel. Jaime and Beau were enjoying their new baby, a little girl. We didn't have to be at the airport until later that afternoon. Stopping at the desk as we walked in, I asked for a late checkout and it was granted with no problem. We were still in our wedding attire. I could tell by looking at Lucy that she was exhausted.

She walked into the elevator and I followed behind her. The anxiety was flowing off of her like a strong perfume. Rubbing my hand over her exposed upper back, she leaned into me. I kissed the top of her head. She was my wife. And I couldn't have been any happier. The elevator opened to our floor and we walked out. She let me lead the way and when we reached our room, I swooped her up in my arms.

"Not so fast, Wife."

She giggled as I opened the door while balancing her in my arms. Walking into the suite, I set her down once we walked a good way inside. She tried to suppress the yawn, but wasn't able to and I followed suit.

"Come here." She hesitated, but walked to me. Cupping her face, I kissed her forehead. "I had so many things in mind for you, but they'll have to wait. We should sleep. We have to be at the airport by four."

She smiled at me and wrapped her arms around my waist. Her words were muffled, but I understood them. "Thank you. I know how awkward this must be."

"It doesn't need to be."

I felt her tip her head up and met her gaze. Her eyes were a unique shade of blue and striking even though she was sleep deprived. She surprised me when she got on her tip toes and kissed me. I wasn't sure I'd ever get used to her showing me affection. Slowly, I sucked on her lips. We were finally alone. My hands on her face and in her hair, I savored her. I wasn't going to push her, she had to initiate things, though I was already rock hard for her. Her mouth opened below mine and her tongue met mine. God, I loved kissing this woman. We had years of kissing to make up for starting right now.

Breathless, she pulled back and smiled shyly. She was flushed and moaned, though I wasn't sure if it was in desperation or annoyance.

"Come on. Let's get you out of this dress." Her eyes bulged slightly and I grinned. "So you can sleep. I won't push you, Lucy, no matter how bad I want you." She studied me for a moment before nodding her head and turning around. The corset back stared back at me, taunting me, and I had no idea where to start. "Umm, how do I get this off?"

Her hand reached around and pulled on some strings that were hidden at the bottom of the corset. "Here. Just have to keep loosening it until I can manage to step out of it."

"Ok." I was so worried my big hands would damage the dress. Working carefully, I began the process of loosening it. As it started to fall open, her back exposed to me, I saw immediately that she wore no bra. Christ! "You're not going to make this easy on me are you?"

Turning her face, she glanced at me over her shoulder. "Sorry. I can take it off in the bathroom, I just need my bag."

She pointed to her suitcase and I said, "Hang on." I grabbed the bag and set it on the bed. "I'll give you a few minutes." She nodded as I began unbuttoning my shirt as I walked out of the bedroom.

Removing my jacket, I threw it over a chair and smiled. We did it. Lucy Roberts was now my Lucy Kerrigan. I checked my phone and found some texts from my brothers. Most were inappropriate and I expected nothing less from them. I spotted the bottle of champagne and two glasses that waited for us. There was a card next to it and I picked it up. Noticing the ice was melted, I put the bottle in the fridge.

With the card in hand, I made my way back to the bedroom. "Lucy? Can I come in?" There was no response and I poked my head in to find her sitting on the end of the bed, half asleep in a tank top and shorts.

Setting the card down, I walked over to her. She had a few hair pins in her hand and was trying to pull more out of her hair. Pushing her hands out of the way, I climbed behind her and removed the hair pins for her.

"Thank you."

"It's no problem. Just relax." Her shoulders slumped as she let me take over her task.

Once I pulled the pins out—there must have been close to thirty—I took them all from her, placing them on the night stand. I began rubbing her shoulders, causing her to coo. "Oh, God. That feels amazing." I continued massaging her shoulders before I started up her neck and over her scalp. "I'm totally going to fall asleep on you."

"Wouldn't be the first time. Go to sleep. I got you."

A few minutes later, her back totally relaxed against my chest, I noticed the change in her breathing. She was asleep. I should've moved us to the head of the bed when she was awake. Now I was afraid to move her. Good thing she was so small. I waited, hoping she was in a deep enough sleep, before I moved her. Scooping her into my lap, I stood with her in my arms and walked to the side of the bed. Somehow I managed to pull the covers back and laid her down.

Brushing the hair from her face, I covered her up, and then stood and stretched. The sun was peering into the room and I closed the drapes and turned on the fan to create some white noise. Stripping out of the rest of my clothes, I stood in the middle of the room in nothing but my underwear. Oh well. She'd get used to it. I made sure the 'do not disturb' tag was on the door and walked back to the bedroom. I crawled in next to her, trying to keep my distance.

When I woke and rolled to face her, I found her in the middle of the bed with her back to me. Unable to resist, I placed my hand on her hip.

"Heath?" It was barely a whisper.

"Shh, go back to sleep."

"You can come closer."

"You sure?"

"Shut up and hold me before I change my mind."

Chuckling, I wrapped my arm around her and nestled her into my body. Right where she belonged.

Waking to her fingers running over my torso was an unexpected surprise. I was on my back and her head was on my chest, just under my chin. I decided to lay still and let her have her fun, wondering how daring she would be. A finger swirled around my navel and then over the ridge of muscle at my hip before moving up to my nipple. It wouldn't be long before she noticed the tent in my underwear.

It was growing increasingly harder to feign sleep. Her leg slid up my thigh and found the evidence of my morning wood. She was torturing me on purpose, I was convinced of it. I couldn't stand it anymore.

"Lucy..." She nearly leapt off the bed when I said her name. Well, I botched that. "Sorry. I didn't mean to startle you."

"How long were you awake?"

Smirking at her and rolling to my side I stared at her. "Long enough."

Her hands covered her face as she mumbled out, "Oh, God." Before I could stop her, she slammed a pillow in my face. "Jerk!"

If she wanted to have a pillow fight, I'd happily oblige. Grabbing the pillow she'd just nailed me with, I threw it back at her. She squealed, covering her face as the pillow struck her. I jumped on top of her, knees on each side of her hips and began tickling her.

"If I remember correctly, you're quite ticklish."

Totally dead pan, she replied, "No, I'm not."

As my hands continued I could see her resolve fading. "Yes, you are. Just need to find the right..." she started squirming as I found the spot by her inner hip, "...there it is."

"Ah!" She fought under me for a moment before begging for me to stop. "Heath! Ok, ok, stop... Ah! Please!"

Removing my hands, I folded them over my chest as she caught her breath. She was a vision. Seeing her this way would never get old. I watched as she pulled a clump of hair from her mouth that'd been caught there during my tickle attack. Slowly, I leaned down to her, bracing my hands on the bed. The sexual tension was building and we both knew it.

Pushing the hair back from her forehead, I whispered, "Good morning, Wife."

She smiled up at me, "Good morning, Husband."

I shifted my arms to lie on my forearms, my face now mere inches from hers. "I'm going to kiss you."

Her pupils reacted ever so slightly as she toyed with me. "It's about time."

Groaning, I took my time getting closer and closer to her lips. Her tongue glided across them and slipped back into her mouth as she pressed her lips together. Her eyes closed as I moved in closer and when my lips almost touched hers, I kissed her nose instead, and then her closed eyes. I followed with her cheeks, forehead, and across her jawline, down to her neck. Her breathing was growing erratic. I spotted her hands gripping the sheets before they moved to my forearms.

Working her ear over with my teeth and lips, I asked, "Did you want me to kiss you somewhere else?" I moved to lie between her legs, careful not to crush her. Like a reflex, her legs bent at the knee as I nestled myself between her legs.

"No. That's pretty good." Her answer surprised me, but she was good at that. Always surprising me.

"No?" I moved back to her jawline, "So, not here?"

"Unh uh." She may have tried to hide it, but I felt her hips arch up slightly seeking out my body.

"You lie."

Before she could respond, I silenced her with my kiss. She moaned into my mouth, her tongue eagerly awaiting mine. I let my weight fall on to her a little more as my hands roamed her body. Down her side and over her thigh before moving back up to trace the ridges of her collar bones. Her hands moved up my arms and around my neck as my own crept under, between her and the sheets.

Worried I would crush her, I wrapped her up tight in my arms and pulled her up with me as I sat on my knees. My hands slipped under the fabric of her shorts where they met her thighs and squeezed. I could feel her nipples pressed against my chest as she squirmed in my arms. God, I wanted to bury myself inside her so bad. I'd had a hard-on for her for ten years. Finally, the moment had arrived.

"Lucy." She wiggled against my cock making it extremely difficult to think. "Lucy, please. I want to do this right. If you're not ready, tell me now."

She pulled back and stroked my face. "I'm ready." I couldn't contain the smile that spread across my face. "Make me yours, Heath." She kissed me before I could respond.

My hands pushed under the back of her tank top when the piercing tones of the hotel phone rang through the air. FUCK! She stiffened in my arms as I pulled my mouth from hers and looked to the clock.

"Shit! That's our wake up call." Her head dropped to my shoulder as she groaned. "Baby, believe me, I understand. I don't want our first time to be rushed. I want to savor you and I'm not going to have you miss out on your honeymoon. We have to be at the airport in two hours and it's an hour drive."

She sniffled and it caught me off guard. Pulling her face up, I saw that she was crying. "I'm sorry. I'm just, ugh!"

"I'll make it up to you. I promise. Seven days just you, me, and the beach." I kissed her forehead as the hotel phone rang again. I reached and snagged the phone, "Yes! Thank you!" Slamming it back down, I looked back to my beautifully disheveled wife. "Seven days and then a whole lifetime. I promise. We just have to wait one more day." Nodding, I kissed her lips quickly. "Go take a shower."

~ CHAPTER 13 ~

~ HEATH ~

After putting our luggage in the trunk of the cab, we climbed in. I pulled the card out of my pocket and handed it to her. "Hope you packed your bathing suit."

Her eyes got all big as she opened it up. "Key West?" I nodded. "God, I hope it's warm!"

"It's only December, let's hope it's still warm!"

We spent the rest of the evening in the air and in airports, with one layover. When we finally got to Key West it was pretty late. We checked into the resort and were showed to our room, which turned out to be a suite. Tipping the bellboy and closing the door, I found her on the balcony. We had a view of the ocean and it couldn't be more perfect.

Inhaling deeply, she smiled at me. "This is amazing."

"Have you been to Florida before?" She shook her head before curling into my side. "Really? Well, I'll make sure you have a good time...in and out of the room."

"Mmm. I'm sure you will." She barely managed to get the words out as a yawn overtook her.

"Come on, let's get you to bed. We have nowhere to be tomorrow and you need a good night's rest."

She didn't put up a fight. When I tucked her into bed, she almost instantly fell asleep. I changed my clothes and lay down next to her for far too long. Sleep never came and I decided to venture to the hotel gym that was open 24/7. After working out for an hour, covered in sweat, I went back to our room. Checking on her, I found her still sound asleep.

Turning the shower on, I climbed in and let the water beat down on me. My cock taunted me, standing at half-mast. I stroked him diligently before stopping. This wasn't the release I was patiently waiting for.

"Can I help?"

I froze at the sound of her voice and lifting my head, I saw her looking at me through the clear upper portion of the shower curtain. Yes. No. How did I respond? I was at a loss for words as my cock grew harder. She pulled the curtain aside and locked eyes with me before she examined my body.

"Lucy..."

"Heath..."

She pushed the shorts down her hips and I watched as they dropped at her feet. Scanning my eyes up her legs, my eyes fixed themselves on the white panties that read 'Bride' on the small front panel. Groaning, I continued lifting my eyes and spotted her nipples beaded against the fabric of her shirt. Reaching down, I turned the water off and stepped out of the shower, now our body's mere inches apart. Her chest heaved as I closed the distance, until she was backed up against the counter.

"Heath..."

"Lucy..."

Neither of us seemed to be able to manage any other words. Picking her up, I set her ass down on the counter and stood between her legs, my cock jutting out between us. Her breasts, I was dying to see them and so I grabbed the bottom of the tank and pulled it over her head. They were small and perfect, nipples pointing up and begging for attention.

She was trembling, hands resting on the counter as I pushed the hair out of her face. My fingers moved over her collar bone and then down the center of her chest until they ran over the string waistband of the panties she wore. Her sharp intake of breath turned me on even more. Gripping them, she lifted up so that I could remove them. My lips dropped to her neck and worked down to her breasts. Laving attention on both before moving to her navel. One hand moved over my neck and shoulders as the other reached for my dick.

Moaning, she begged, "Heath, please."

"Soon."

As I worked lower, I felt her lean back, resting on her elbows. Her scent filling the air had me intoxicated. She had a small landing strip and was bald everywhere else. Trailing my arm down her calf until in encircled her ankle, I placed her foot up and on the counter before doing the same with the other.

"Oh, Jesus." She was nearly delusional and I hadn't even begun. This was going to be fun.

Gripping her ass, I moved her to the very edge of the counter and began kissing over her mound. Dipping my tongue down, I found her clit and circled it gently as she moaned and tilted her hips closer. Pulling her lips in between my own, one after the other, before licking at her again, her wetness becoming more unmistakable. Slowly, I tongued her pussy before pulling out and closing my lips around her clit. Humming, she trembled further and began cursing.

"Please, Heath."

"Shut up, Lucy and let me taste you. Every. Part. Of. You."

Groaning, her head dropped back against the mirror as I slid a finger inside her while my thumb circled her nub. Standing, I grabbed her by the back of the neck with my free hand and brought her closer to me.

"Do you know how delicious you taste?" She shook her head and so I pulled my finger from her body and circled her lips with it. Without reservation she sucked my finger into her mouth, scraping her teeth over my knuckles. Taking my finger back, I returned it to her pussy and added a second finger. "I can promise you one thing, Lucy," her eyes fluttered open and focused on mine, "you're going to be sore when I'm done with you. And, I'll never be done, so I hope you're ready to be sore forever."

Her eyes closed as she panted, "Promise."

"I promise."

She yanked my mouth to hers and kissed me frantically. "Make me yours, please. I want to be yours."

"Hold on to me." Her legs flung around my waist as I carried her to the bedroom. Yanking the covers aside, I laid us down on our sides as we kissed and groped each other. "Let me grab the condoms." She nodded as I left the bed and grabbed the box of condoms in my suitcase.

After pulling a few free, I set them down on the side table and she eyed me with that smirk of hers. "Really? Going to need all of those are you?"

"Probably more. Those should get us through the next couple hours." She started to say something and I stopped her, "Shut up, Lucy, before I prove to you that Heath *is* your flavor of choice, and not caramel."

"I might be up to that challenge."

Grabbing her ankles, I pulled her close and turned her over. Slapping her ass right before kissing it, then I worked my way up her spine. "I think someone's craving my Heath bar." Biting at her flesh, the goosebumps flitted across her skin.

Sucking on her neck, I then grabbed her hair and lifted her face toward mine before closing my mouth over hers. She managed to roll over under me and pulled me close, my dick throbbing against her body.

"If you don't take me right now, I'm going to make you regret it." She bit onto my lower lip and sucked hard while I tried reaching for a condom. Releasing me, I snagged the condom and rolled it down my length in a frenzy.

Moving between her legs, I lowered myself down and kissed her as our bodies aligned with one another. My tip slid over her lips and to her entrance with the guidance of my hand. I ran my dick up and over her again as she cooed in pleasure, arching her back. When I did it again, she bucked her hips and my head sank into her.

"Lucy, look at me." Her eyes flickered open as I pulled out and sank in a little deeper. "You're so beautiful."

Panting as she smiled, she said, "You are, too." Lifting her hips, she took all of me as I dropped my mouth to her neck. "Heath, you feel amazing. Please, kiss me."

Not one to deny her, I stroked her face and kissed her until we were out of breath. Gently rocking against one another, I picked up my pace once our lips parted. Pulling out and grinding back into her, her head thrashed against the bed as her hands clawed at my body. I wanted to make it last and fought the urge to blow my load. Kneeling up, I took her hands in mine and pulled her up to me.

Gasping as I sank into her again, she dropped her forehead to mine as her breath mingled with my own. Cupping her ass, I moved her up and down my cock as she gripped me tightly. Her arms tightened around my shoulders and her kiss became fevered.

"I got you, Lucy."

"Pah, please. Don't stop."

Rolling to my back, I kissed her mouth before whispering, "Take what you want. I'm not coming until you do."

Moaning, she slowly began to ride me. When she sat up, her hair a mess, eyes hazy, lips swollen, and her cheeks flushed, staring down at me, that's when I fell entirely. No other woman had ever meant anything. It'd always been her. No other kiss meant what hers did. No other touch, no other look, and on and on. I wanted to make her, and only her, feel this way forever.

After a few moments, she lowered herself again, kissing my neck while her hips moved in harmony with mine. Her movements became repetitive and I suspected she was close. Gripping her back, I held her close and then moved my hands to her face.

"Look at me angel." She looked like a different Lucy. Panicked, frantic, possessed, and lips slightly parted as she gasped for breath.

"Heath, I'm close. Come with me."

Smiling, I reaffirmed, "I'm going to make you mine and then I'll cum."

"Oh...mmm." She moved faster and gripped me so fiercely, I knew I couldn't wait much longer. "Heath!" Her nails dug into my shoulders as her orgasm flooded her, her body tensing and flinching at every touch.

Bucking my hips to give her every inch, I groaned out, "You're mine. Don't stop, Lucy." Her movements had begun slowing, but when I spoke she rocked on me furiously.

"Cum for me, Heath. I want you to cum."

"Ahhh." Gripping her hips, probably tight enough to bruise her, I pumped in and out of her and my seed burst through me. "Lucy!"

"I got you." She squeezed her walls around me, not stopping until I was motionless below her. Dropping down on top of me, she continued pulsing around my softening dick.

Wiggling against me, I pried her off of me and rolled on top of her. "You were amazing and I suspect you want more, but I need a few minutes to recover."

"What are you offering?"

My fingers moved over her soaking lips as she mewled into my mouth. "What do you want?"

"I don't know how much more I can take."

"You can always take more. I'll be gentle."

Moving lower, I licked and stroked her clit until she was writhing below me again. Crawling back up the bed, I pulled her limp body into my arms. We didn't speak, just slept. When I woke, it was to room service delivering our breakfast.

~ CHAPTER 14 ~

~ HEATH ~

Once the smell of breakfast infiltrated the bedroom, she began to wake. I had swiped a piece of bacon and began waving it under her nose.

"Rise and shine, beautiful."

Stretching out like a cat, under the sheets, she smiled at me before pulling the covers over her exposed chest. Leaning down, she kissed me hesitantly. Cocking my head at her, she seemed to sense my question.

"Sorry. Morning breath and all."

"And all?"

"It's been a long time since I woke up with someone and you're not just someone. You're you, Heath, my husband."

"You didn't seem to mind this morning." She missed the teasing in my voice and became nervous. "Relax Lucy. We both have things to get used to and I'm looking forward to that." Smirking, unsure if she was having regrets or just becoming accustomed to her new title, I suggested, "Well, you should get dressed. Breakfast awaits."

After breakfast she took a shower and got dressed and I did the same. She was being guarded and I wasn't quite sure why. We needed to talk about some things, but we had all week. Fun and getting to know her were what I had on the agenda. As much as I cared about her, we didn't know each other like we should and the thought of it excited and terrified me.

We spent the day shopping and strolling the beaches. When we got back to our room, she plopped down on the bed and yawned.

"Why don't you take a nap? I need to get a workout in."

"I shouldn't. I'll be up all night."

Raising a brow at her, I agreed. "Yes, yes you will."

With hooded eyes, she scanned my body and questioned me. "You going to give me a workout, Heathcliff?"

"Depends what you're looking for." Leaning over the bed, my face hovered over hers. "Cardio, strength, endurance, what's your poison?"

Groaning, she huffed, "I keep forgetting you're a gym rat."

"Hey! I resemble that remark." I winked at her so she'd know I was playing along.

Giggling she shook her head. "Meat head!"

"Play nice, Lucy. Will and I are quite successful." Will and I owned a few gyms and we're looking at other locations to start up. He handled more of the behind the scenes business side while I handled the employees and clients.

Rolling her eyes at me, she rolled over. "Wake me when you're done."

"Will do." It was quite evident that she worked out, but had refused to accept a membership at our gym years ago. Well that was going to change. I couldn't have my wife working out with the competition. It was bad business.

After my workout, I found her passed out face down in the bed. Stripping my clothes, I climbed in next to her, running my hands over her back and down her legs.

Mumbling, she stirred, "You stink!"

"I came to mark my territory."

"You're disgusting." At the same time she reached her hand back and quickly found my arousal. "And horny, apparently."

"Apparently." She stroked me for a moment and I conceded, "I'll go shower real quick."

"You don't have to." Rolling to face me she confessed, "There's something sexy about a hot sweaty man."

We were frenzied and deliberate with our fucking and I promised her better after we got some food in us. We showered together before getting ready for dinner. I'd made reservations for us at a well-known restaurant and we both dressed up. She wore a dress with amazing strappy heels and I knew I'd be the envy of any man who saw her.

Once we were seated at our table, I asked if she wanted wine. "What do you prefer; red, white, blush?"

"Moscato, white. I'm not a big fan of dry either." I ordered a bottle and when the server left the table she teased me, "I think you're trying to get me drunk again."

"Well, of course I am. We both know what happens when you're drunk."

Totally dead-pan like only she could, she left me speechless. "If you want me to suck your cock all you have to do is ask." I couldn't figure her out. One minute she was reserved and timid and the next she was seducing me. "Cat got your tongue?"

Shaking my head, I took a sip of my water before I answered her. "I can't figure you out. That's all." Narrowing her eyes, she wanted more of an explanation. "One minute you're hot and the next you're cold."

"I am not cold!"

Oh, shit. Not the reaction I wanted. "I didn't mean it like that." I reached for her hand, but she pulled it back before I could grab hold of it. "Lucy." Scooting my chair closer, I whispered, "I didn't mean it like that. I know we're still trying to figure each other out. I'm sorry."

"It's a lot. I'm sorry, too. I think I'm so used to sparring with you, that it just comes naturally."

"I agree. We both need to work on bringing our defenses down. How about we play a game?"

Smiling, "Game?"

"Like twenty questions or truth or dare. We can take turns." She agreed and I put the ball in her court. "Ladies first."

"Should we set some ground rules?"

"Like?"

"Um, I don't think we should discuss sexual exploits in great detail. I don't need to know who you have and haven't slept with."

"I was a virgin until yesterday." Her eyes expanded and I couldn't contain my laughter.

"Shut up! See, you can't even be serious."

"I'm sorry. Ok. I agree, but I like the idea of *you* being a virgin until yesterday."

Snorting, she quipped, "You can think that all you want, Heathcliff Kerrigan."

Groaning as jealousy surged through me at the thought of her sleeping with other men, I agreed, "Ok. No sexual exploits involving names and numbers of said sexual conquests."

"Agreed." Pursing her lips, she examined my face. "Ok Mr. Romantic. What's the most romantic thing you've ever done?"

"Hmm." There hadn't been many grand gestures of love in my past. "I made some mixed CDs for a girl once. Does that count?"

"Aww. Yes, that counts! Did she like them?"

"I don't know."

"What do you mean you don't know?"

I couldn't tell her that the CDs had been made for her and that I was too chicken to give them to her. "That was two questions. Now it's my turn." The server brought the bottle and filled our glasses as I thought about what to ask her. "What was it about Will?"

"Heath."

"It's just a question."

"Isn't it obvious? You were always so mean to me, and, well, he wasn't."

"Don't you know that being mean is how boys show that they like you?"

"Horse shit! That was two questions. My turn." I waved my hand at her, encouraging her on. "Where do you live?"

"Don't you know?" She shook her head. "Will and I live above our gym, the first one off 5th street." Now that I said that out loud, I knew that living arrangement would never work. "Guess I don't anymore."

"We can find a new place together."

"I'm easy. I can move into your place, too. I don't mind."

"My lease is up in January. I didn't renew it, with the wedding and everything."

"Shit. Ok. Guess we need to find a place." That wouldn't be so easy given that we were approaching Christmas.

"Sorry. I didn't think anyone would want to live in my dinky apartment."

"It's ok. Really. We'll figure it out. Hell, we can make Will find a new place if need be. He can crash at O's or we can, while he's deployed. It'll be fine."

We ordered dinner and spent the entire time filling each other in on the years and gaps we'd missed in each other's lives. A second bottle appeared on our table, courtesy of management, and we didn't hesitate to enjoy it. It was getting late and when I looked around, we were one of the very few couples left on the terrace. Propane heat lamps kept the space warm. The sky was littered with stars and music played overhead.

"Dance with me." She simply nodded as I offered her my hand. *Only You* by Matthew Perryman played overhead like I'd arranged with the restaurant staff. She let me hold her close and with her heels adding to her height she was able to rest her head in the crook of my neck. "I wouldn't change this for the world, Lucy. I've only ever wanted you."

Pulling back, she looked to me and smiled. She was thinking about something, I was sure of it and I was sure I wouldn't like it. "Why?"

"What do you mean why? Stop thinking so much. You think too much."

"I know I do." Listening to my advice, she tucked herself back into my body as I held her tighter. I was beginning to feel guilty about the secret I was keeping from her, but there was no way I could tell her. But I also knew I couldn't keep the secret from her forever.

Pushing it down, I danced and held her while a few more songs played. We walked back to our room and spent the next several hours doing what all newlyweds on their honeymoon should be doing. I couldn't get enough of her and each time I had her I just wanted more.

~ CHAPTER 15 ~

~ HEATH ~

After a week of wonderful in Key West, we were headed home. When we landed, got our luggage, and hailed a cab, we both became silent when the cabby asked for the address.

"Let's swing by my place and then we can drive over to your place. I'll pack a bag. We won't have any privacy at my place." Smiling, she agreed. Placing her head on my shoulder, I pulled her legs over my lap as she curled into my side for the cab drive to my place.

When we pulled in front of the building, I took her through the gym entrance after paying the cab driver. Walking to the front desk, I pulled out some paperwork for her and handed it to her.

"What's this for?"

"Membership. I can't have you going to the competition." She glared at me and I smiled. "It's free. Consider it a perk of being married to one of the owners."

Rolling her eyes she grunted her approval. "Fine. If you don't offer the same classes we're going to have a problem!"

"Tell me the classes and I'll make it happen." She narrowed her eyes at me and I winked.

Stella walked over just then and got a little too touchy with me like she usually did. "Heath! Where've you been? I missed you."

Will and I hadn't told anyone at work that I was married, wanting to see first how things developed. And given the fact that Will hated dealing with the employees directly, it was clear he still hadn't told anyone.

"He's been with me. On our honeymoon." I blew out a breath, trying to contain my amusement at Lucy's statement of ownership.

"That's funny. Heath married?" Stella glared at Lucy while snickering, doing what any insecure chick did and took in her appearance.

Lucy with her ivory skin and piercing blue eyes, was petite in every way, appearing delicate, yet she was anything but. Stella was average height, voluptuous, and had olive skin that matched her eyes. And her tits were fake. I wasn't picky, but preferred my women all natural.

Stella still had her hand on my arm when she added, "Honey, you're not his type."

Stella couldn't have been more wrong. Lucy *was* my type, *she* wasn't, not anymore. I kept silent, curious what Lucy would say and do and I wasn't left waiting long.

"And what *type* would that be?" She returned Stella's stare, scanning her up and down as she spit out, "Pretty sure floozy isn't Heath's type."

Stella removed her hand from my arm and braced her hands on the counter as she leaned in closer to Lucy. "Pretty sure bitch isn't his type either."

"That would be Mrs. Bitch to you." Lucy just smiled and then stretched out her hand to Stella, "Mrs. Lucy Kerrigan. Who might you be?"

Stella was speechless and I was worried she may jump across the counter at Lucy. While the thought of them in a cat fight was appealing, I didn't need the added drama. When it became evident that Stella wasn't going to shake her hand, Lucy dropped it back to her side, still smiling.

"Lucy, this is Stella. One of my instructors."

"Seriously. You're married?" I just smiled and nodded. She grabbed my left hand and found the ring. Lucy held up her finger and Stella dropped my hand.

She stormed off as Lucy quipped, "Pleasure to meet you, Stella." When Stella was out of ear range, Lucy's smile dissipated and she narrowed her icy eyes at me. "Ex-girlfriend?"

Shrugging my shoulders, "I wouldn't necessarily give her that title."

"Nice. So you sleep with the help. Anyone else I should keep an eye out for since I have to work out here now?"

I wasn't sure how to answer that. I knew about my reputation for sleeping with my instructors and maybe a few clients, too.

"Jesus Christ, Heath! How have you not been sued for sexual harassment?"

Defending myself, I smirked, "They all pursued me!"

"Really? You're going that route?" She rolled her eyes and started looking around the gym. We were both being stared at, men and women alike. Turning back to look at me over the counter separating us, she announced, "He's married and I'll cut a bitch. Got it?" Most of the men just smiled and laughed whereas the women looked offended and went back to their routines or left.

I walked around the counter and put my arms around her waist, "If you just cost me customers we're going to have a problem." I smiled at her and she just smiled back.

"Happy wife, happy life. If those tramps are here to get lucky with you, they can go elsewhere."

"So possessive. I like it."

She smacked my arm. "Knock it off. But, seriously. I'll cut a bitch. Better yet, I'll shank a bitch." She cupped my cheeks that were again covered in a short beard and said, "Mine," before kissing me.

"You're back!"

We turned to find Will staring at us. "Yup. I needed to grab some things and then we're headed back to her place."

Looking between us, he added, "Well, there are some pressing matters we should discuss when you have the time."

Running my hand through my hair, I wasn't quite sure what to do when Lucy spoke up. "It's fine. I can wait."

"It's not a five minute thing." Will seemed irritated so I knew something was up.

"Ok." Turning to Lucy, I suggested, "Why don't you go back to your place? I'll be there in a few hours."

She agreed as Will added, "I can drop him off if you want to take his car."

"That's a great idea." Turning to Will, "Give me five minutes. I'll meet you in the office." He nodded and walked away without saying another word. Pulling out my keys, I handed her the keys to my car. "It's the silver one." Dangling them in front of her, I warned, "Don't get yourself killed."

Tilting her head, she inquired, "What is it?"

"Fast. Here." I grabbed her bags, leaving mine at the desk and walked her to the back lot. "Leave it in the trunk if you want. I can get it when I get there."

"I'm not helpless Mr. Kerrigan."

"Oh, I know. You'll shank a bitch. Got it!" We both laughed as I popped the trunk and put her bag in. "Ok. Here you go." I tossed her the keys as she smiled devilishly. "Don't. Get. Killed."

"No. But I can't promise I won't get pulled over!" Opening the door for her, I swatted her ass. She started it up once she buckled in, and the purr of the engine filled the air as she revved the engine. "Damn. This is going to be fun!"

"Bad girl. Just take it slow coming in and out of parking lots. The front is lower than you think."

Tipping her hand away from her forehead she mocked me, "Yes, Sir!" She started playing with the radio, synced her phone, and scrolled through a playlist before picking a song. "Here...just for you!"

I looked to the display and saw that *Bad Girl* by Avril Lavigne was the song she selected. "I'm going to choke you if anything happens to her."

"I don't mind a little choking." Winking at me, I was speechless. She just laughed as she backed out of the spot and cranked the radio louder. She waved to me in the rearview mirror and squealed the tires as she pulled out of the parking lot.

Making my way inside, I grabbed my bag and headed up to the massive apartment Will and I shared. It was a huge open space with two separate master suites at opposite ends, with the kitchen, office, and living space in the middle. We kept a lot of the industrial feel it had when we remodeled, since it had once been a warehouse. Steel beams and lots of glass were primary features of the space.

Carrying my bag to my room, I dropped it on my bed and then started packing another. Will's figure appeared in the doorway and I continued packing, knowing he'd start talking soon enough.

"Montrose may be a problem."

"What? We scouted it for months. It's the perfect location." Montrose was where we were hoping to open our fourth branch and what we needed if we wanted to continue branching out.

"Apparently we're not the only ones interested in the property. And Jameson's nephew is friends with Steve."

"Fuck!" Jameson was part of the building commission in Montrose and Steve was the owner of another local gym branch. Our competition. "Do we have any ins?"

"Stella."

"Christ."

"I'm guessing she's pretty pissed about your marital status. I just found her cussing out the new receptionist and she had her in tears."

"She's a fucking irrational basket case."

"Well maybe you should've thought about that before you fucked her."

I ignored his comment. I wasn't the only one with skeletons in my closet. "So what do we do?"

"I don't know. I have a lunch scheduled with Jameson on Wednesday. If you could make it, I think it could really help."

"Yeah, sure. Tell me when and where. If I have clients, I'll reschedule them."

Nodding, he thanked me, "Great. Thank you." He didn't leave and I caught his stressed habit of rubbing the back of his neck and then the bridge of his nose. "So, Lucy. Did you talk to her?"

"I'm not discussing my wife with you. We're in a really great place, considering how everything went down."

"She's going to find out. And if it doesn't come from you…we'll both have hell to pay."

I was growing frustrated and took it out on my bag. Tossing it aside I growled out in frustration, "I'll handle it. I can't lose her. Not now."

"The longer…"

"Will! I got it."

Inhaling deeply he mumbled, "I hope so."

He started to leave my room and I stopped him. "Hey, what are the odds of you finding another place? Lucy's lease is up at the end of the month and I figure the three of us here isn't the best scenario."

"Dude, I don't know. We shouldn't really be taking out any more credit until we figure out Montrose. I don't want to jeopardize it any further."

Nodding and looking around my room, I tried taking it all in. I knew he was right. "Maybe we'll crash at O's for a few months."

"I might be willing to do that, too. His place is closer to Montrose."

"Ok. We'll figure it out. I should get going."

He slapped his hand on my shoulder and congratulated me. "I really do hope this works out with you and Lucy. I know what she means to you and I hope she knows it too." I just nodded my head and he left the room while I finished packing.

~ CHAPTER 16 ~

~ HEATH ~

Calling Lucy before Will drove to drop me off, I offered to pick up dinner and she agreed. I stopped and picked up a pizza. Will carried up the pizza while I juggled my bags. When the door flew open, we didn't expect what we saw.

Lucy stood there in red lingerie, practically see through. She looked smoking hot. I forgot Will was standing behind me until her eyes practically bugged out of her head, her cheeks as red as the scrap of fabric she wore, and she ran to the bedroom.

Dropping my bags just inside the door, I took the pizza from my brother. He smiled and shook his head and headed down the hall. "Go get her, tiger."

I shut and locked the door without responding. Setting the pizza on the counter, I started walking toward the bedroom. Just before I reached the door, it flung open and Lucy wasn't wearing the lingerie anymore.

"Whoa, whoa. What's this?" She was wearing sweats and still seemed frazzled.

"You could've warned me he was coming up." Her hands were on her hips as she scrutinized me.

"Umm, you could've warned me! Go put that back on."

She sashayed right past me, flung the lid to the pizza open and pulled a slice out. With a smile full of grit she bantered, "Not a chance."

Lucy pulled some plates out of the cupboard and waters out of the fridge and offered me one of each. She walked over to the couch and made herself comfortable. Grabbing the bottle of water, the box, and setting my plate on top I sat down next to her after placing the pizza down on the coffee table.

We sat and ate quietly and I couldn't stand it anymore. "So, I'm not sure I can look for a new apartment space right now." She looked at me and I knew she had the wrong idea. "I want to, it's the business. We're in the middle of obtaining another property and I can't secure another debt right now, not until that's taken care of."

"How long will that be?"

"Hopefully just a couple months. Will said he might be willing to stay at O's place, it's closer to the new site for him.

We could stay at my place. It's big, I think you'd like it." She just shrugged her shoulders. Something was bothering her. "What's wrong, Lucy? Talk to me."

She looked at me warily, "I, it's stupid."

"Tell me."

Sighing, she let it out, "I don't know if I can live there and not think about all the women before me. In your bed, in that apartment."

She was jealous and I was too. She'd had men before me, but I wasn't about to let it get in the way of us. "Lucy, they're in the past. You've had men here, too, and it doesn't bother me." She just shook her head at me. "What are you saying no to?"

"I've never brought a man here. Only you." I had to force my mouth shut after my jaw dropped. "It'd been almost two years since I'd slept with anyone. I'm guessing that's not the case for you."

"Um, no." She sat silent and I was fucking lost as to what I should say and do. Those women were all in my past. I only wanted her. "You can make the space yours. Whatever you want. Unless we can find a way to renew here."

"It's already been leased. I'm being ridiculous. We can stay at your place. With or without Will, and when we can, we'll re-evaluate our living situation. I just want to take it one day at a time."

Smiling, I set my plate down and invaded her space on the other end of the couch. "You make me smile, Lucy Kerrigan." My hand moved up her leg as she leaned back, trying to avoid my face hovering over hers. "I know your weakness. Don't make me tickle it out of you."

"Tickle what out of me?"

"That! That smile of yours." She rolled her eyes and smiled brightly. Softly, I whispered, "I love that smile. It taunts me in my dreams." I kissed her nose and then her cheeks.

Her breathing was increasing as she asked, "You dream about me?"

"All. The. Time."

I let my mouth hover over hers before dropping my lips to her neck. Moaning, she whimpered my name, "Heath…"

Her fingers ran over the back of my neck and over my scalp, pulling me closer. Dropping my weight onto her, she slid lower until she was on her back, under me. Reaching my hand under the sweatshirt, I found silky material beneath it. Looking down, I found the red lingerie she'd been wearing at the door.

"You didn't take it off." She just shook her head. Pulling the sweatshirt over her head, I took in the sight of her. "Up you go." Moving off of her, I pulled her to stand in front of me while I sat on the couch. I made eye contact with her before slowly pulling the sweats off her hips and down her legs. "Damn."

The red lingerie against her skin was a sharp contrast. My hands moved up the back of her legs, cupping her exposed cheeks. The things I needed to tell her started running rampant through my head. I didn't deserve her. Wrapping my arms around her, I pulled her close, resting my head against her belly.

"I don't deserve you."

Her hands were moving through my hair, "Yes, you do. I don't deserve *you*." She moved to climb into my lap, straddling my waist and gazed into my eyes. "All these years I've never given you the time of day. I'm sorry." Her voice was showing signs of cracking and I shushed her.

"That's in the past. I agree. Let's just take everything one day at a time."

"Kiss me."

"It'd be my honor."

The kiss wasn't rushed, it was slow and passionate. She was an amazing kisser and it took all my brain power to remember to kiss her back. Hands roamed and teeth nipped as we fondled each other. Pressing herself into my erection, I dropped my head back and pushed up against her as she moaned.

She yanked my t-shirt over my head, running her hands over my torso as my muscles flexed in reaction to her touch. Her hands sank into my pants and my hungry cock awaited her. She stroked him only the way she could as I lay back, watching her eyes on mine. Her lips turned up slightly as I began moving my hips in rhythm to her hand.

"Shit. I can't take this much longer. I need to be inside you, Lucy." I didn't wait for an answer, just stood up with her in my arms and carried her back to her room.

It was the first time I was really seeing her room. I'd only checked on her once that night all those months ago and it was dark so I couldn't see much. She had a queen sized bed with matching furniture. It wasn't girly in décor, but more modern than I thought she'd be, with a few bright accent colors. Dropping her to the bed, I stripped off my pants while kicking off my shoes and pulling off my socks.

Pulling my phone from my pants, I pulled up my playlist. Selecting *Animals* by Chris Call. It was an unplugged version and quickly becoming one of my favorite 'Lucy' songs.

~ CHAPTER 17 ~

~ HEATH ~

It was Christmas Eve. I had worked a twelve hour day and wanted nothing more than to get home to her. We were planning to spend Christmas morning together, alone, and then we would head to my family's place where her parents would be, too. We'd only been married a few weeks, but they'd been amazing and I wouldn't have changed them for anything.

Sitting in my car, my radio presets had been changed again. She'd changed them all for the first time that day she drove my car to her place after the honeymoon. I was convinced she would change them whenever she was at the gym.

Texting her, I chastised her for changing them AGAIN. She just responded with a wink emoticon and a heart. She's lucky I loved her. Not that I'd said it to her yet. My phone chimed again and it was her.

#wannatasteMYheathbar

I laughed and my dick twitched. She was horny and it was her way of telling me so.

When I walked in the door, I didn't hear or see her. Maybe she wasn't home yet. Strolling into the bedroom, I found her standing by the dresser in nothing but scraps of lace. Finding her this way would never get old.

Nodding toward the bed, she told me to sit down and I did as she said. "Get over here, woman!"

Giggling, she teased me, "Hold your horses. I just wanted some music."

She put on *Ride* by SoMo. It wasn't the first time she played music while we got naughty and I didn't mind. The song was a huge turn on for her and that was a turn on for me. We even started a playlist of bedroom songs while in Key West, which was my idea and she went along with it.

Sitting on the edge of the bed, she walked over to me and began swaying to the music. She began dancing for me and I thought I might die. I'd joked about it in Key West, but she just shrugged it off saying she was no dancer. Her ass was rubbing against my lap and I couldn't resist touching her.

"Ah, ah. No touching." She winked as she turned to face me and backed away.

My hands itched to touch her and gripped the bedding next to me instead. If she was no dancer, I thought her a liar. "You've been practicing."

Smiling, she confessed, "I've been taking classes with Stacey."

"What other secrets are you keeping from me?"

"Guess you'll have to wait and find out."

It'd become so easy for me to lose myself in her the past couple weeks. She was all I thought about day and night. A dream I never thought could come true. I watched the fabric pull and flutter over her skin with her movements as her muscles flexed. She was breathtaking as she flashed that smile and those diamond blue eyes at me over her shoulder. I was completely at her disposal and would do anything for her. Whether she knew that or not, I wasn't sure.

Turning to face me as her hands ran over her torso, she moved closer with her eyes downcast. With my hands gripping the bedding behind me, I leaned back and took her in. Moving to stand between my legs, she bent down, her breasts brushing against my thighs as her hands gripped my knees. She moved and stood so that her perfect ass was staring me in the face. Unable to keep my hands to myself, I ran my hands up the front of her thighs to her hips and over her belly, trying to pull her closer.

"Tsk, tsk Mr. Kerrigan. Don't make me call security."

Groaning in protest, I released her as she moved away from me with a smile on her lips. "Lucy." Her smile just got bigger as she beckoned me, with the curl of her finger, to come to her.

When I was halfway to her she put her hand up to stop me and I obeyed, reluctantly. She danced around me, her hands dancing over my hips and below my waistband. Standing behind me, she pushed her hands under my shirt and ran their softness up to my shoulder blades and then around to my chest. Reaching back down, she grabbed the hem and pulled it up. I finished yanking it off for her as she moved to face me again.

I tried to speak and she shushed me and then pulled my mouth down to hers. The rush of something foreign ran through me and I wasn't sure how to explain it. It was like a craving I'd never experienced. I wanted to consume all of her and didn't know how to ever quench my thirst for her. I couldn't keep my hands off her anymore.

Picking her up, she let out a small squeal as I raised her up until my arms were fully outstretched. Staring down at me, she looked like an angel with her platinum blonde hair framing her face. I quickly wrapped my arms around her as she slowly slid down my body. When her face was inches above mine, she cupped my cheeks and I closed my eyes in response.

The kiss was slow and passionate, but soon her legs circled around my torso as she pressed herself closer to me. One hand at her neck and the other on her ass, my hand squeezed roughly eliciting a moan from her. As our kiss deepened and became more frenzied I became more impatient. Breathless, I sat back down on the edge of the bed with her still clinging to me. I had to tell her, I should tell her.

"Heath, I..."

"Yes?" She seemed unsure as she searched my eyes. "What is it, angel?"

"I just..." her eyes closed before she dropped her head to my shoulder.

Pulling back so I could see her, I cradled her face in my hands, and pleaded with her. "Tell me, please. You can talk to me. I'm not going anywhere."

Searching my eyes and pulling her upper lip between her teeth, she confided in me. "I just want you to know how happy I've been these past couple weeks." She paused and I knew if she just said the words, I would say them back without hesitation or remorse. "I've never felt this way."

Smiling and playing with her hair, I echoed her sentiment, "Me, too."

Whispering against my lips, she said the three words that made me lose my control. "Make me yours." They weren't the words I was hoping to hear, but they were a close second. Maybe it was her way of telling me she loved me.

Rolling over, I dropped my weight on her as she relaxed into the bed. Lifting her arms, I had her grip the headboard and warned her, "Don't move." Her eyes closed and her back arched in response.

Letting my hand move down her arm, over her underarm, I watched as she bit her lip trying to avoid laughing. She was very ticklish and we'd spent a good amount of time overcoming that. Gripping her neck gently, the way she liked, I pulled her lower lip between my teeth. Grinding my pelvis into hers, she mewled out her desire.

Growling out what I knew she loved hearing, "Mine." She released a breath, like a surrender, and gave herself over to me.

Kneeling up, I pulled my sweats and boxer briefs down in one motion. Holding her ankle, I kissed up her leg until my face was buried between her legs and nipping at her through her lace panties. They were damp with her desire and I easily slid them off her. Reaching under her back to remove her bra,

I slid the cups up to expose her breasts. She knew not to let go of the headboard as I moved the bra up her arms.

"You can take it off, then put your hands back."

I loved seeing her body stretched out for me. Legs resting on top of mine, her nipples puckered and pointing to the ceiling, she was the most beautiful thing I'd ever seen. Sucking her breast into my mouth while my fingers pinched the other nipple, her pants of pleasure were like music to my ears. Stretching my arm out, I pulled open the drawer where we kept the condoms.

"Heath." Turning to her, she surprised me with her request. "No barriers, not anymore."

A million things ran through my head. I had told myself I wouldn't remove the barrier between us until she told me she loved me, when and if she ever did. I know that it was silly, but it was what it was.

Sensing my hesitation, she alerted me to information I wasn't aware of. "I have an IUC, there's no risk of a baby. Not until…we're ready." The thought of having kids with her elated me, but nothing was 100% safe and I wanted a few years with her before I gave up part of her to our kids. "I trust you."

"I trust you, too. It's not that." She stroked my face. "It's purely selfish of me. I don't want to share you with anyone, not even a baby. Not yet."

Leaning up, she kissed my lips. "I love how sweet you are. You're something else, Heathcliff Kerrigan." Not me, just how sweet I was. "Stop overthinking and make love to me."

~ CHAPTER 18 ~

~ HEATH ~

She lay back down, wrapped her hands around the headboard, and smiled at me. Fuck it. I'd pull out, if I could manage it. I wanted to feel her the way it was meant to be. Kissing her neck and all the way down her body, I drove her to the brink with my tongue and stopped before she fell over the edge.

Smiling, I leaned over her face as she cursed me. "One day you're going to wake up tied to the bed with me sitting on your face, you fucking tease."

Shrugging my shoulders, I encouraged her, "Sounds like a good time to me." She started to speak and moaned instead when I slid into her. Momentarily forgetting I wasn't wearing a condom, I groaned my appreciation. "Fuck, Lucy.'

"Yes, I know. Fuck Lucy. Now!" Rocking back, I sank into her all the way as a shiver passed over her. "Heath, kiss me, please."

Kissing her, my hips moved in and out of her with deliberate intention. Running my hand up her arms, I pried them from the headboard, and she flung them around my neck. Nails digging into my shoulders, her teeth nipped at my neck and my ear.

"I, oh, God. Don't, yes." She was speaking in tongues and I kissed her into silence.

"Relax and breathe. Let it consume you the way you consume me."

I felt her relax around me as she tried to catch her breath. Gripping my cock tighter, her breath came in quick bursts as she cried out. "Don't stop, not till you cum."

I did just that, pumped in and out of her as her whole body flinched underneath me. Just before I was about to cum, I pulled out and her hand covered my own as my seed shot all over our hands. With her other hand, she pulled my mouth down to hers and kissed me until the sensations ceased. After cleaning up, we slept naked and tangled around one another and made love a few more times that night.

We woke Christmas morning to the sound of our phones ringing. We'd slept most of the morning away and I wanted nothing more than to turn our phones off and hide away with my wife.

We exchanged gifts and I loved what she got me. Some clothes and a watch that she had engraved with 'To Heath, my new favorite flavor.' I wouldn't be able to show the engraving to anyone and loved it even more because of that. Bravely, I got her some more lingerie and some diamond studs. When she opened the earrings, she seemed genuinely surprised and put them right in. Promising to model the lingerie later, we got ready to head to my family's place to enjoy the holiday with our families.

I was in the basement at the bar with my brothers, minus O who was still deployed. D'Artagnan wandered off and Dorian brought up the subject I was worried he would. I tried to get him and Will to drop it. It was the last thing I wanted to deal with or discuss, especially on Christmas.

"Heath, man, I understand, but Dorian's right. You have to tell her the truth."

"The truth about what?"

We all turned around to a stone faced Lucy. Slowly D and Dorian left and Will stepped to the other side of the room. I took a few steps toward her and took her hand. This was the last thing I wanted and especially not on Christmas. I knew I had to tell her, I just wanted to get through Christmas and get us moved into my place, which we were planning to do after New Year's.

"Lucy, I, shit."

"Heath, you're scaring me. What's going on?"

"I'm not your match." I just spit it out and waited for her wrath.

She started laughing, "Yes you are. Stop messing around." She glanced over to Will and then back to me and the looks on our faces must've given it away. She blinked and questioned me, "What do you mean?"

"I'm not your match. You were supposed to marry Will. Not me."

She blinked and began mumbling. "But how, what? I don't understand."

Will walked over and began talking and I was grateful, for once, for him interjecting. I couldn't even process everything he was saying, my attention fully focused on Lucy. Her face paled and then she started turning red. Her hand released mine and started clenching at her side. Will finished telling her and the three of us stood silent for a few minutes, waiting for her to say something, anything.

Turning her back on us, I could see her body shaking. Will and I exchanged a nod and he started to exit the room, leaving me alone with Lucy. Stopping in front of Lucy, he began to apologize to her and was met with a slap to the face.

"I don't want your apology!"

"Lucy." She turned on me just as quick and smacked me, too.

"Who all knew? Everyone? Is this another prank? Jesus. How could you do this to me again?" She was pacing the room and Will had disappeared.

"Please let me explain."

She was nearly delusional, laughing and screaming at the same time. "Explain? How about you explain to me how it is that I fell for your act all over again? I thought…"

She didn't finish her statement and I had to ask, "You thought what?"

Stopping, she stared at me and broke my heart with her words. "I thought I was falling in love with you. How could I have been so wrong?"

"Please, you're not wrong. Everything between us is real. Lucy, I lov…"

"NO! Don't you dare say that to me! You don't know the meaning of the word. You've lied to me for weeks." She started hyperventilating and to make matters worse, my mom came into the room just then.

"Lucy, Heath, what's going on?"

"Please. Like you don't know?"

"She doesn't know, Lucy."

My mother looked between the two of us and demanded, "Know what?"

I couldn't find the words and Lucy outed me out to my mom, not that I blamed her. "It seems that I was supposed to marry Will, not Heath. The boys did a switch-a-roo on me once again."

"What? Once again?"

"That summer, ten years ago. They did the same thing, only I thought I was spending all my time with Will to find out it was really Heath."

"Honey, of course it was Heath. He's been in love with you since you were a little girl."

"Mom!" Looking to Lucy, she looked ill. "You're not helping mom."

"Son, is this true about the wedding? Please tell me it's not." I didn't have to say anything for her to know the truth.

"Heathcliff Daniel Kerrigan. Get out of my sight while I talk to Lucy."

"Mom."

"Now."

I looked to Lucy, but she refused to make eye contact with me. I left the room and grabbed a drink before I locked myself in the back bathroom. I couldn't begin to imagine what my mother was telling Lucy, but I prayed that it helped. The events that led up to the wedding began running through my head once again.

I'd just gotten home and found Dorian and Will in the kitchen talking. As I approached, I realized it was a heated discussion.

"Everything ok? We still going out tonight. Big day's tomorrow, Will!"

Dorian glanced at Will and shook his head. "You can't marry her, Will."

"Don't you think I know that? Christ."

"Chickening out, huh?" I drank my water and waited for my brother's reasoning for cold feet.

"It's Lucy."

Choking on my water, once I could speak again I questioned them. "What do you mean it's Lucy?"

They explained that Dorian put the pieces together earlier that day. Dorian was business partners with Lucy's brother and he'd let it slip to Dorian. Dorian then called the hotel where one of the staff members confirmed that the Roberts Kerrigan wedding was taking place the next day.

They knew how I felt about her and how Will had never felt that way. Will was ready to confront her and call the whole thing off. Me, I'm the one who decided the wedding could still take place. Will and Dorian being the supportive brothers they were, went along with the plan. I ran to the nearest jewelry store and bought the anchor necklace. I was on cloud nine as long as we could pull it off.

When the justice of the peace showed up at the hotel the next morning, our plan was made even easier. The marriage certificate didn't have Will's name on it, so I was able to put my name. Now I just had to convince Lucy to follow through with it when she saw me standing at the altar waiting for her. I was still worried that if given the choice between Will and myself, I'd always be the loser.

"Son." My mother's voice carried through the door and I opened it. "I can't believe you and Will did this to her. And don't get me started on that prank ten years ago. I raised you boys better than that."

"I know. Where is she? I need to try to explain, make it right."

"She left."

"What do you mean she left?"

"Heathcliff, she's incredibly hurt and confused. You need to give her some space to sort through her feelings."

"The hell I do. She's my wife!"

"Yes, she is. She loves you, I truly believe that. But you've crushed her with your secret. You need to give her time."

"I can't. I have to see her."

"You're not going to find her, not right away."

"What did you do? Dammit mom!"

"I'm not going to tell you where she is, not until she agrees to see you. I love you and if you weren't grown I'd consider taking the belt to you." The tears began to fall as my mom pulled me in her arms. "Have you told her you love her?"

Shaking my head, I replied, "No. Mom, please tell me where she is. I have to tell her."

"I won't, not yet. Trust me. You need to give her time. She's your wife and that can't change overnight. Have faith in what you've built, even if you built it on false pretense." She sighed and asked another question I hadn't thought of. "Why didn't you and Will just tell her the truth and let her decide?"

"Because I've never believed she'd pick me."

"You're a fool Heathcliff. That girl loves you. Always has."

Will drove me back to the city a couple of hours later. I'd tried calling and texting her and got no answer. My car was parked in her parking lot, but her car was gone. When I made it up to the apartment, I prayed she'd be there, knowing she wasn't. Drawers were open in the dresser. Evidence that she'd clearly left in a hurry. Her toothbrush and other toiletries were all gone, too.

Grabbing a bottle of liquor from the kitchen cabinet, I sat on the bed and stared at my feet before downing a good portion of the bottle. All I wanted to do the rest of my life was honor her with a love she'd never known and one she'd never want to let go of. Now I was worried I'd lost her for good. I prayed my mother was right, that Lucy was in love with me and would come back to me.

I woke the next morning to someone banging on the apartment door. My head was pounding from the copious amounts of alcohol I'd ingested. Walking to the door in just my underwear, I flung the door open.

It was Will.

"What's going on?" He looked like he'd seen a ghost. He couldn't form words and looked like he'd been crying. "Is it Lucy? What's going on?"

Shaking his head, he croaked out, "It's O."

My heart plummeted. I couldn't take much more. O was on another tour of duty and we all knew the risks. I wasn't sure if I was going to be able to handle what Will was about to tell me.

LOVE

~ CHAPTER 19 ~

~ LUCY ~

We were spending our annual Fourth of July week up at the Kerrigan's cottage. I was seventeen, had just graduated from high school, and my boyfriend Jon had driven up to spend the week with me. He was bunking with the boys, which came with its own set of concerns. I wasn't exactly sure who he was rooming with—I didn't want to know—but the five boys shared two bedrooms and Jon made number six.

"So, why didn't you tell me that you and Heath were an item once?"

I balked at Jon, not sure what to say and wondering who had told him anything. Our vacation was half over and I didn't want to fight with him. So I lied. "What are you talking about? Heath and I have never been an item."

"He knows about your birth mark."

Huffing at him, "Of course he does. I've known his entire family my whole life. There are pictures of me as a baby running this beach naked." I glared at him as he digested my words. "Are you done?"

He nodded and apologized. "Sorry. He just seemed rather convincing."

"He's jealous. Forget about him."

We went for a walk and ended up at the boat house. Heath had been getting on my nerves all week with his little comments to me. He didn't like Jon, that was obvious, and I suppose he had every right not to. Me, I was too blind in my disdain for Heath to listen about his warnings in regards to Jon. I slept with Jon that night, in the boat house, giving him my virginity. The next morning Jon was gone and I never heard from him again.

I stood outside the Kerrigan lake house as the memories continued to assail me.

Heath and I actually had a good conversation a couple days later, the day before we were all set to go back home. He'd put the pieces together—well, some of them—and caught me in a moment of vulnerability.

"He doesn't deserve you, Lucy. I'd never do that."

"Do what?" I laughed, trying to hide my hurt about the whole situation.

He pushed some hair behind my ear and leaned in. Scared of what he was about to do, I grabbed his beer and took a swig. Choking on it and making a disgusted look I handed it back to him.

"How can you drink that? It's nasty."

Shrugging his shoulders, he retorted, "It's an acquired taste."

He was eyeing me in a way that made me nervous. My stomach fluttered and my heart raced. I did the only thing I knew how to do. I ran.

I used the key Mrs. Kerrigan had given me and made my way inside. I'd swung by my apartment and packed a small bag. I had to be back to work in a couple days, so whatever I came here to figure out, I needed to do it soon. I hadn't been to the lake house in several years and I found that not much had changed.

I yearned to put my feet in the sand and wished it was summertime. Shivering, I turned up the thermostat and followed the directions to turn the utilities back on. Wandering through the house, I found myself in the room Heath always stayed in. The bedrooms the boys shared were large with two sets of bunk beds built into the walls so that the rooms could sleep four.

The emotions flooded me as I remembered us on that bottom bunk, kissing as teenagers. Slamming the door shut, I made my way to the back of the house which had always been designated as *my* room. My phone was going off like crazy in my pocket. Pulling it out, I saw several missed calls from Heath. Resigning, I turned it to silent and put it on the dresser.

Pulling the space heater out of the closet, I plugged it in before changing my clothes. I needed to sleep. Making sure the house was locked up, I crawled into bed. I woke the next morning to Mrs. Kerrigan calling my name.

I sat up in bed as she opened my bedroom door. "Morning dear. I don't want to bother you, but I wanted to give these to you."

Blinking the sleep from my eyes, I watched her set down a couple CD cases. What time was it? Had I slept in that late or was she that early?

"What's that?"

"I was up all night looking for them. They're for you." She sat down next to me and took my hand. "I know what they did was wrong, but please know one thing." I nodded when I realized she was waiting for me to agree before she continued. "He loves you, to the brink of stupidity, he loves you."

Disagreeing, I proclaimed, "He doesn't. He's never said it."

"Lucy," she smiled serenely, "the brink of stupidity." She stood and let me know there was a CD player in the master bedroom and then left. By the time I got my body to function to run after her it was too late. I watched her car driving down the drive and then she was gone.

Dragging my feet, I walked back to the bedroom and stared at the CDs sitting on the end of the bed. Huffing, I ignored them and headed to the kitchen. The fridge had fresh groceries and I knew she must have brought them. Some fruit, half a gallon of milk, some eggs, cheese, and other necessities would help me survive for a few days. Pouring myself a bowl of cereal, I curled up in front of the TV.

Realizing I'd been watching TV for hours and not paying attention to it, I turned it off. All I could think about was him. When had this happened? When had I fallen so completely for him?

Grabbing the CDs, I headed to the master bedroom and found the CD player. Remembering that the master bath had a large Jacuzzi tub, I decided to indulge. Running the bath water, I looked over the CDs. Opening them, I found notes scribbled inside the cover dated ten years ago.

Lucy,

If I had enough courage to give you these, I'm sure you'd give me a chance. I'm sorry I ever hurt you. Please forgive me.

Heath

I started tearing up immediately. The CDs he'd talked about making while on our honeymoon were made for me. I put them in order and placed the first one in the player. Turning the bath water off, I hit play and sank into the whirlpool tub.

Our wedding song played first, like a punch to the gut. Knowing I was alone, I let the tears flow. How could I forgive him? How could I not? Nobody had ever done anything so romantic for me. *She Will Be Loved* by Maroon 5 came on next. It was hard not to fantasize about how my teen years and young adulthood would have been different had I been in a relationship with Heath the whole time.

My skin wrinkled, the water cooling, and the first CD over, I crawled out of the tub. My emotions and sensibilities fighting with one another. The songs were all so meaningful and a couple really hit home with me. Picking up my cell, I noticed it was entirely dead. Digging through my bag, I realized I didn't bring my wall charger. Shit! I got dressed and plugged it in to the charger in my car, knowing it'd take forever.

I left my cell in my car and decided to sleep on it one more night. I'd go home in the morning and make my decision. I knew I had to talk to Heath and give him a chance to explain. He deserved that much no matter what my decision was.

~ CHAPTER 20 ~

~ HEATH ~

I showered in a fog and got dressed while Will waited for me. Lucy, while ever present in my heart and head, had to be put on the back burner. My family needed me. Packing my bags, I left Lucy a note telling her I'd be back. Of course I still didn't know when she'd be back or where she was.

Popping some ibuprofen, I grabbed a protein bar and headed out the door with my brother. Glancing in the apartment, I couldn't help the feeling of foreboding that fell over me. Praying I was just closing a chapter and not a book, I shut the door behind me.

When we got to my parents' house, my mother was clearly distraught and my father was doing all he could to console her. Speaking with Dorian, there wasn't any more info. We knew that O had been seriously injured and we were waiting for more information. The call had come earlier that morning and we discovered that my mom hadn't even been home when the call came in. It didn't occur to me to ask where she'd been so early in the day. Our dad had to tell her when she got home.

When the phone rang a couple hours later we all paled. Dad answered it as my mother clutched his hand. After a few minutes and writing some things down, he hung up the phone.

Taking a deep breath he eased our minds. "He's alive. They're transporting him to NYC. He should be there tomorrow."

"Thank God."

"There's something you all need to know." We all stared at him, not sure what to expect him to say. "He's lost his left leg at the knee."

My mind seemed to fall into a freefall at that point. O was alive, but he'd lost his leg. I was thankful he was alive, but I couldn't begin to imagine what he was going through and would continue to go through.

"Heath, are you ok?" Looking to my father, I just nodded. "Do you want to come? I know how close you and O are."

"I'm sorry. What?"

"Mom and I are going to drive to NYC in the am. Do you want to come?"

"Yes, of course. I'll come."

The next morning we were packing up when my phone began ringing. Looking at the screen, I saw that it was Lucy. I ignored the call, I didn't have the energy to deal with her. If she could ignore my calls for a day, I could do the same. As I was loading our bags into my parents' car, Will came out.

"Heath," he motioned me closer and I obliged. "It's Lucy."

My heart sank. "What do you mean it's Lucy?"

"She's at the lake house and stuck on the side of the road. They're getting nailed with snow and apparently she was on her way home."

"Christ! I can't deal with this now."

"She's your wife. You can't leave her on the side of the road in the middle of a snowstorm." I stood and contemplated what to do. I wanted to be there with O, but Lucy could be in danger. "I can take my truck and go get her, but I think you should come with me."

"Yeah. I got it." I pulled my bag out of my parents' car and asked them to drive safe. "I can't believe you let her go up there knowing what the weather is like up there this time of year!"

"Heath! We understand, but don't take it out on your mother." Dad clapped me on the shoulder and added, "We'll be in touch. O will understand. Go make sure Lucy's safe."

I overheard Will on the phone with Lucy, trying to figure out where she was. Throwing my bag in his backseat, we headed up to the lake house. A few hours later, we were finally almost there. The drive had taken three times longer than it should have.

"You said she was here. I don't see any tracks." I was growing panicked at the thought of not finding her.

"It's been several hours, Heath. Her tracks are long covered. Try calling her." Digging out my phone, I dialed her. She answered and she was clearly shaken up. "Lucy, where are you? We don't see your tracks. Can you honk the horn or flash the lights?"

I could sense the terror in her voice as she confirmed that her car was out of gas and the battery was close behind. The call was disconnected and that's when my anxiety began to take over. We weren't more than ten or fifteen minutes from the lake house and it was clear no one had been driving on the roads in hours.

"Dammit! What the hell was she thinking?"

"Calm down. We'll find her. And I would gather she was trying to get home. To you." I grunted as we both searched for her, driving extremely slow. "There! Is that her?"

"What the hell is she doing outside of the car?"

"Calm down, Heath. You're going to scare her."

As we approached, I jumped out of the truck and ran over to her as the snow pelted both of us. "What the hell are you doing up here?" She just shook her head. "Why did you try driving home in this? What is wrong with you?"

She was shaking and all the color was lost from her face, but it didn't stop her temper. "Screw you! I didn't do this on purpose!"

"Doubtful. You didn't hesitate to call Will to save the day."

"After you wouldn't answer your fucking phone!"

"Now you know what it's like!"

"HEATH!" I turned to Will as he grated out, "Are you two fucking done? You're acting like children." I knew Will was right, but I wasn't about to agree with him. "Get her in the car. Her lips are blue. NOW!" Opening the back door, she climbed in after grabbing her bag out of her car. "We're going to have to try to make it back to the lake house. It's our safest bet."

"Great."

I took my place in the front seat as Will headed toward the house. We could hear her teeth chattering and I tried to ignore it. My anger convincing me she was getting what she deserved.

"Jesus Christ. Heath, if you don't get back there and warm her up, I will."

"What are you talking about? She's fine."

"Get your head out of your ass." I looked back to her and observed what Will began yelling at me about. "She's fucking blue, her feet are probably wet, and her hair is soaked. She needs to get warm before she gets hypothermia." Grumbling, I climbed over the seat, using Will as a brace. Pushing off his head, he spit out, "Watch it! It's probably going to take at least thirty minutes to get up there."

Lucy put up a small fight, but she was no match for me. "Stop fighting me. Come here."

"There should be some blankets behind you." Glancing into the third row, I found the blankets he was referring to and pulled them to my lap. Running my hands over her clothes, I discovered she *was* soaked and her hair wasn't wet, it was frozen and beginning to thaw in the warmth of the truck.

"Christ. Get these off, Lucy. How long were you standing out in the snow?"

She didn't say anything as I started removing her clothes. I began with her boots, if you could call them that, to find her socks soaking wet and her toes various shades of blue and red. Getting her pants off was a struggle, but I managed. Once she was next to me in just her shirt and panties I wrapped a blanket around her. Knowing she needed my heat, too, I quickly removed my coat and shirt and pulled her into me. I flinched when her cold, wet skin touched mine.

"Th, thank you. I'm s, sor, sorry."

"You could've been killed." Catching Will's glance in the rearview mirror, he nodded and returned his eyes to the road. "It's ok. We just need to get you warm."

We made it to the house and Will had to get out and clear a path to the front door. Once he'd done that, I pulled her to my lap and told her to hang on. With the blanket wrapped around her, I carried her into the house and back to the master bedroom. Will was turning the utilities back on and had already cranked the thermostat.

"You should probably get her in the tub. I'll start a fire and get the space heaters going." I just nodded as I sat her on the bed and walked to the bathroom.

"This might hurt." I'd made the water as warm as I could without risking burning her. I removed her shirt and panties, trying to control my urge to touch her. She stood on trembling legs, naked, in front of me as I helped her into the tub.

Dipping a foot in, she pulled it right back out. "It's too hot!"

"It's not, you're just cold. Get in." Shaking her head, she refused. "Dammit." I started kicking my shoes and pants off as she stared at me in disbelief. "You can make this easy or you can fight, but I'm getting you in that tub."

She made an attempt to dart for the door and was met with Will. Screeching, she slammed the door in his face. Turning on me she hollered, "What is wrong with you two?"

"I'd listen to him, Lucy. He's more patient with you than I would be." I could hear Will's laughter growing more distant, probably because he'd left the bedroom that was on the other side of the closed bathroom door.

Lucy stared at me and when I offered her my hand to help her in the tub, she refused. Brushing past me, she sank herself into the tub, I began climbing in across from her. "Oh, no! You're not getting in this tub."

Smirking, I dictated, "Yes, I am." Pulling her knees to her chest, I climbed in across from her and stretched out, happily invading her space. "Besides, we need to talk."

Her body didn't move, but her eyes peered at mine over her knees. "So talk."

She wasn't going to make it easy, but I liked that about her. You'd think I'd have that figured out by now. "Lucy, never was it my intention to hurt you. I never wanted to hurt you." She sat quiet for such a long time that I was beginning to think all hope was lost. "What are you thinking?"

Closing her eyes and shaking her head slightly, she responded, "My goal going into it was to find *my* match. You took that from me. Now I'm so confused that I don't know what to do." She wiped at her face and I realized she was crying silently. I did this to her. "I care about you. About you both."

"Right. Always Will." I stood up abruptly, splashing water all around us.

Crying out, "Heath! Don't. That's not what I meant." Her hand clutched mine as she tried pulling me back down to the tub. Sitting back down, I waited and listened. "Will must've been hoping to find his match, you too, or you wouldn't have signed up for it. It all takes me back to the beginning. If you wanted me so much, why didn't you pursue *me*?"

Angrily, I spit out, "I did and every time, you rejected me. You never gave me a real chance, Lucy." She cowered back slightly as my fists clenched below the water.

Softly, she countered, "I could say the same to you. I never thought you wanted more than a one night stand with me."

"Lucy!"

"Heath!" She made the first move, unfolding her knees she scooted closer. "I'm sorry I didn't trust that you wanted more. Contrary to what you may think, I don't want to fight with you." I tried to keep my eyes off her face. Her hands searched for mine under the water and I struggled to resist her.

"I can't do this." I stood up and scrambled out of the tub. "You just left, didn't give me time to explain. Nothing."

"I'm sorry. You're guilty of doing the same thing." She climbed out of the tub and wrapped a towel around her body. I stood, hands clenching the counter and saw her walk up behind me. Softly, a hand fell to my back. "Heath," she was crying, "please."

Her hands circled around me as she laid her face against my back. Closing my eyes, I relished the feel of her body against mine. Whispering, not sure she even heard me, "I can't say no to you."

Grabbing her hand, I opened the bathroom door and pulled her into the bedroom. I noticed the bedroom door was closed and mentally thanked my brother for that. Turning to face her, I stared at the towel hiding her from my eyes. What happened next was purely primal. All my anger, love, possession, and desperation about her and everything with O, poured out of me and it should've scared me and her.

Yanking the towel from her body, I turned her and pulled her back against my front. My hands roamed her body as she lay lax against me, letting me do as I wished. Her body trembled and I knew it was with desire and not from the cold. The room was quite warm and I was grateful for it. Her fingers delicately traced over my hips and thighs as I pressed my erection into her back.

Before I knew it, I had her back up against the wall, and her legs around my waist as I sank into her. One arm wrapped around her and the other braced against the wall as I fucked her. She took every inch and moaned with the pleasure of it.

"Heath, kiss me."

Her blue eyes penetrated mine and the hand I had against the wall moved to her neck. She dropped her head against the wall, silently challenging me on. Gently, my hand circled her small neck as I brought my mouth down on hers. She moaned into my mouth and fought for control of the kiss.

Her fingers brushed against the stem of my cock as she circled her clit. She clamped around me, slowly losing control.

"I want to hear you. Louder, Lucy."

She did as I ordered as I moved us to the bed, her moans of desire filling the room and fueling me on. Setting her down, she huffed as I flipped her over, pulling her hips back and picking right up where we'd left off. One hand in her hair, the other reached around to her clit as her breasts brushed against the comforter.

"If you don't come soon, you'll miss out. Come on me, Lucy."

I felt her give her body over to my ministrations as she clenched around me. Her climax reached, it soon began to cease as mine flooded me. Pulling out, I stroked myself, seed spurting all over the small of her back. I dropped down next to her on my back and closed my eyes.

I must've drifted off because when I came to, she was under the covers and asleep. I wasn't sure if we were ok or not. I typically enjoyed cuddling with her after sex and always took advantage of it. This time I hadn't. Making my way under the covers, I turned away from her, not wanting to wake her.

~ CHAPTER 21 ~

~ LUCY ~

Turning to look at him, his eyes were closed and I realized he was sleeping. Gently, I climbed off the bed and cleaned myself up in the bathroom. Something was bothering him, more than just our fight. He'd never been so, callous—maybe that wasn't the word I was looking for—with me in bed. I narrowed it down to the fact that we both needed sleep. We'd have time in the morning to talk more. So I crawled under the covers and tried to do just that.

A few minutes later I felt him stir. Feeling the covers move, he got under the covers, but made no attempt to touch me. Something was horribly wrong. This wasn't the Heath I was used to. Maybe it was too late. I shook the thought away and focused on sleep.

When I woke in the morning, the bed was empty beside me. I got dressed and found Will in the kitchen, but there was no sign of Heath. Will put some pancakes on a plate for me and I happily accepted them. I was growing worried and finally asked Will where Heath was.

"He's with the tow truck pulling your car out."

"Oh. Ok."

An hour later, Will asked if I had everything. We'd started packing back up, in hopes to head back to the city. "Yes, is Heath back?"

He just shook his head. "He took your car to the city. He asked that I take you home."

I was hurt and baffled. "I, but. Ok." Will didn't say anything and soon we were on the road back to the city. I could tell something was also bothering him and asked. "Will, what's going on?"

He glanced over to me and then back to the road. "Did he talk to you about O?"

Confused, I shook my head no and replied the same. "No. What's going on?" Dread filled me and I knew something was appallingly wrong and it involved O. My imagination went crazy knowing the danger O faced fighting for our country.

"He's been injured. Heath was headed out of town yesterday with Mom and Dad to the hospital he was transported to when you called."

Covering my face with my hands, I didn't know what to say. O was more than just a friend, he was like a brother to me. I could only imagine what his family was feeling. "How bad is it?"

Will gave me as many details as he had. As we made it back to the city, the snow wasn't nearly as heavy as it had been at the lake house. The streets were plowed and life was continuing as usual. My car was gone, but Heath's was parked next to my empty spot back at my apartment. I had to work in the morning and New Year's was fast approaching. Apparently I would be using Heath's car.

"Thanks for the ride, Will."

"No problem. You have keys to his car?" I nodded. "Ok. See you around."

"Will?"

"Yeah?"

"Please call or text me if you hear anything."

"Will do."

I ran into Stacey in the hallway and she sensed that something was wrong. Following me to my apartment I spilled everything, like diarrhea of the mouth. She listened and supported me, but was careful not to criticize Heath.

"Lucy, what are you going to do?"

Shaking my head, I was honest. "I don't know. I, I'm falling for him, Stacey."

She smiled, "You fell for him a long time ago. Glad you're finally realizing it."

I tried to object but knew it was pointless. She was right. Had everyone seen it but me? Why had it taken me so long to realize? I wanted Heath. Will was just a distraction, who, being his twin, looked just like him.

"I'm an idiot."

Giggling, "Yeah, well."

I threw her a dirty look and exclaimed, "Bitch!"

Shrugging her shoulders, "That's why you love me." I just shook my head at her. "So, he lied, but tell me about everything else. Tell me about the good."

I couldn't help but smile. There was a lot of good. "He's amazing. I never knew, but he's so romantic." She scrunched her face up and I clarified, "In a good way. He's amazing in bed, like, wow!"

"Dammit! He's hung isn't he?"

Laughing, I egged her on, "Like a horse!"

"Of course he is!"

"I was hurting all week on our honeymoon. In a good way."

"Ugh. I need that kind of pain in my life!"

"Yes, yes you do!"

We hadn't hung out like we were used to and I missed my friend. We talked for a good hour about all the things I loved about Heath. She sat and listened like the good friend she was.

"So, are you still going to move into his place next week?"

"I mean, I hadn't really thought about it. I assume so."

"What do you mean you assume?"

I told her what had happened up at the lake house— leaving out the details of him taking me against the wall— about how he'd been gone when I woke. Then I told her about O. I confided in her that I was worried for Heath and how he'd deal with O's injuries. I was worried about O, as well, but Heath and O were really close, maybe closer than Heath and Will were.

"Just be patient with him. It's hard watching someone you love go through something so painful. Especially when he was doing it protecting and serving our country. My cousin is a therapist near Montrose and works with many injured vets."

I tucked that piece of info away and checked my phone. There were no missed calls or texts from him. I couldn't help but worry that he didn't feel the same way I did. Maybe my leaving on Christmas night had set us back further than we could recover from.

"Lucy, he'll be back. I've seen how he looks at you. He's not going anywhere, but you're probably going to have to prove that you aren't either." I nodded and she added, "So. Let's order take out and watch movies. Just like we used to."

"Yes!"

It was New Year's Eve and I still hadn't heard from Heath. Will confirmed he was in New York, with his parents and O. I texted him to let him know I was thinking of him and that if he needed to talk, I was there. I was hurt that he wasn't responding, but I tried to be considerate of the situation.

Because of the holiday, I had just gotten home from a short day at work. My apartment was in boxes and I was supposed to move to Heath's in two days. There was a knock on my door. Still in my scrubs, I answered and saw Will, Dorian, and D'Artagnan standing there.

Baffled, I asked, "What's going on?"

Will answered my question immediately. "Hope you're done packing. It's moving day." I shook my head at him with my silent question. "Heath, O, mom, and dad are coming home in a couple days. We won't have time to move you then. It's now or never. How much do you have left? We have two trucks and your car."

I corrected him, "Heath's car." I didn't need the reminder that he'd left town with my car and not a word to me.

Ignoring my comment, he looked around and determined, "You look about done."

I blew out a big breath, "Um, ok. We had planned to put my living room furniture in storage, but my bedroom furniture is going to his place."

"Yup. Heath said the same thing. We already put his bedroom furniture in storage this morning. Once O gets settled at home, I may move in with him."

It was like a slap to the face. Heath was talking to his brothers, but not to me. He was going to get an earful when I finally saw him. I changed clothes real quick and boxed up my remaining items.

Within a few hours, we were unloading my stuff at Heath and Will's place. Dorian and D'Artagnan took my furniture to the storage unit while Will helped me put the bedroom together. It was a little weird setting up our bedroom with my husband's twin brother instead of him. But, everything about the situation had already surpassed weird.

I couldn't avoid the topic any longer. "Will, so you didn't know it was me? Not until..."

He perked up and looked at me. "No. Not until the day before." We both stood silent and I realized being in his presence alone did nothing for me, except remind me of Heath. "His heart was in the right place. I never would've been able to go through with it, not with you."

"No, I know." We didn't say anything else. I think we were both slightly uncomfortable and knew that it was a discussion I should be having with Heath.

I invited Stacey over, but she had a date and I didn't want to take that away from her. Will had left and I was left alone. Before he left, he gave me the code to the back stairwell that lead down to the gym. Since, apparently, I had nothing better to do, I decided to get a workout in. Wearing my workout clothes and with a bottle of water in hand, I headed down.

Their gym was open 24/7, but since it was a holiday, the gym was virtually empty. I got on the elliptical and with my earbuds in, began climbing away. Twenty minutes later, I was surfing through my playlist. I put on the song that'd been haunting me that I currently loved to hate. *What Kind Of Man* by Florence and The Machine blared in my head.

One kiss between us all those years ago had changed everything. Then another kiss this past summer changed everything again. But, his absence the past week had me on the edge of breaking. How could he do this to me? He promised he wouldn't hurt me, begged me to trust him. I upped the resistance on the elliptical and pushed myself harder. The adrenaline and my anger got the best of me as I screamed out in frustration.

Embarrassed by my outburst, I looked around to see a couple lifting weights staring at me. I just waved and apologized as I made my way to the locker room. Splashing cold water on my face, I tried to get my emotions under control. It was time to call it a night and head back upstairs.

~ CHAPTER 22 ~

~ HEATH ~

I knew I shouldn't have left without talking to her, but I just wasn't ready for the talk I knew we had to have. Will would make sure she got home safe. He'd taken me to her car, with a gas tank in hand, and helped me dig her car out before we parted ways. The tow truck arrived shortly afterward and pulled her car out to the road. I had to get to O. Then it dawned on me that she didn't even know about O. Without meaning to, I'd just made matters worse. I debated about turning around, but couldn't follow through with it.

Several hours later, longer than it should've taken due to the road conditions, I was parking at the hospital in NYC and headed up to his floor. Checking in at the nurse's station, they sent me on back. I knew about his leg, but I wasn't prepared to see him looking as battered as he was.

Bandages covered the left side of his face and arm. The blankets laid flat where they should have been puffed up had he not lost his leg. My dad walked over and hugged me before I even realized they were there. O appeared to be sleeping and I soon found out that he was heavily medicated and had yet to wake since my parents arrived.

A few hours later, O's voice pulled us all from our conversation. "What's a guy got to do to get some peace and quiet around here?" He was attempting a smile and my mom ran over to his bedside and kissed his face.

After my parents got their hellos in, we clasped right hands and nodded at each other. He was hurting, mentally and physically, and trying to hide it. We were told he knew about the loss of his leg, but no one wanted to mention it either. We'd also been warned to expect outbursts from him, which was completely understandable.

My parents had gone down to the cafeteria for dinner and promised to bring me back some food, leaving me with O.

"So, how's married life?"

Trying to cover the uncertainty in my voice, I lied, "It's great. Things are good."

He laughed, "You're full of shit. How the hell did you end up marrying Lucy Roberts? I know it was more than coincidence. Spill it."

He'd missed out on all the details and I resigned myself and told him. I'm sure he could use the distraction and I needed someone to talk to. I told him how Dorian found out and told Will and how I'd walked in on that conversation.

"She said yes, you married her. So what's the problem?" He stared me down and put the pieces together.

"You idiot. You didn't tell her it was supposed to be Will, did you?" He waited and shook his head at me. "How'd she find out?"

"Christmas."

"Nice."

"I tried talking to her, but she left and mom helped her." That got another laugh out of him. "Mom refused to tell me where she was…"

"Probably the lake house."

"Yes, seems everyone was able to figure that out but me."

He shrugged his shoulders, "You're blinded by love. So, have you talked to her yet?"

"Yes, no. Not really."

Our conversation ended when my parents reappeared. It wasn't long before O was sleeping again and my parents were headed to the hotel. I opted to stay with him, since one family member was allowed to stay overnight. Trying to get myself as comfortable as possible on the fold out chair, I checked my phone. Will had gotten her home. He didn't say anything else which was probably his way of warning me that she was pissed.

A couple days later, O was working hard on the crutches. He'd be fitted for a prosthetic when we got him home and fully healed.

"Come on, O. You're doing great." His positive attitude was something to be commended, but I knew him well enough to know how much he was hiding. We were a lot alike in that aspect.

Tomorrow was New Year's Eve and I missed her, though I wouldn't admit it to anyone. I didn't want to ring in the year without her by my side. She'd called and texted several times and I had yet to respond.

"Go home, Heath. You miss her." He caught me staring at my phone again and I slid it in my pocket.

"I'm here for you..."

"And I'm fine. Mom and dad are here. I'll be home in a few days." He sat down and glared at me. "I'm serious. I know Lucy, too. She's going to make you pay for this. Stop stalling."

Rolling my eyes, I conceded. "Yeah, I know. We're supposed to move her into my place next week. Maybe I'll see if we can get it done tomorrow."

"Call her."

The next afternoon, I was headed home. I hadn't called her, but Will, Dorian, and D were moving her today. Shovel in hand, I kept digging my hole deeper. Maybe she wouldn't be as angry as O said she would be. Maybe she'd throw her arms around me and we could forget there was ever a problem between us. Fuck. I should just commit myself now. There was going to be hell to pay, Lucy Roberts style.

I got into town a few hours later and swung by her place. Everything was already cleared out and I was impressed. She must've had a majority of the packing done when my brothers showed up. I took it as a good sign. Parking in the back of my building, I went up to the apartment I shared with Will, and now my wife. Everything was silent. There were some boxes stacked and when I made my way to the bedroom, I found it rearranged with her furniture.

We had agreed to that change, but it would take some getting used to. Though I'd never admit to her that I preferred her mattress to my old one. My car was parked out back, so I figured she was either out with friends or maybe in the gym. Changing my clothes, I headed down to the gym. I'd missed my workouts the past few days and needed to get back at it.

Stopping in the office first, I checked emails and the mail. Everything seemed to be fine when a scream echoed through the walls. What the hell? I got up and went to see what the commotion was about.

I saw her as I turned the corner, but she hadn't seen me. She was swiping at her face, earbuds in her ears, and she looked pissed. I tried calling her name, but it was no use. She disappeared into the locker room. Scrubbing my hands over my face, I leaned against the wall. Dropping my head back, I closed my eyes.

"Trouble in paradise?" Fuck!

Putting a smile on my face, I pushed off the wall and ignored her question. "Hello, Stella. Everything's just fine."

She tilted her head at me and chirped, "Hmm. Guess I'll go see for myself."

"Stella…" I tried to halt her, but there was no stopping her. She was devious and had a nasty streak. Remind me why it was I slept with her? I groaned and waited to see if I'd have to break-up a cat fight in the locker room.

~ CHAPTER 23 ~

~ LUCY ~

As I began to exit the locker room, I ran right into her. I tried apologizing and walking away, not wanting to get into any kind of argument with her.

With snide sarcasm she stated, "Honeymoon's over, huh? I'm not surprised."

My fingernails dug into the palms of my hand as my fists clenched. I continued walking out of the locker room and turned to face her, not sure what I was going to say, when I was quickly silenced by his voice.

"Hey baby. There you are." Heath walked up beside me and draped his arm around my shoulder. I couldn't bear to look at him, but smiled at Stella as I leaned into him. "Stella, if you'll excuse us. We have plans."

She turned on her heels and huffed, mumbling who knows what under her breath. When she was out of sight, I shrugged his arm off of me and headed toward the back stairwell. As I began climbing the stairs, I heard him trailing behind me.

"No welcome home?"

That was it. I'd had enough. Turning on the landing after the first flight of stairs, I screamed down at him, "Screw you! You've been gone for days, ignoring my calls and texts. Then your brothers show up today to let me know that you've asked them to move me today. Not when we had planned, but today. You couldn't even be bothered to tell me yourself."

His arms crossed as he leaned against the wall and quietly observed me. "Are you done?"

"No!" Taking a deep breath, I bellowed, "You left that morning without saying a word. You didn't tell me about O, never muttered a word. You just left!"

His voice was raised as he spit back, "Yes, let's talk about how *I* just left. Not before you did. You wouldn't even hear me out. And don't get me started on O. He's NOT *YOUR* BROTHER."

"How dare you? He's like a brother to me and you know it."

"Just like I was or just like Will was?"

"Ahhhh! Why are you being so cruel?"

Curling that lip he snarled, "I learned it from you."

Reacting, I threw the bottle of water I was holding at his head. His quick reaction had him deflecting it off his forearm. He looked furious and started up the stairs after me. I tried outrunning him, but my legs were mush and soon I was over his shoulder.

"You need a lesson in manners."

"Me? You're out of your damn mind! Someone with manners would answer his damn phone when his *wife* is calling."

Setting me down in front of the door to the apartment, he pushed the code and opened the door. "Wife, huh? You sure that's what you want to be? Because a few days ago it would seem you wanted to be anything but."

"You mean when I let you fuck me in your parents bed at the lake house?" I knew that's not what he was referring to, but I had to get my dig in. "I'm not the one who left that morning without a word."

He stared at me and I shoved past him, making my way to the bedroom. The place was foreign to me and seeing my furniture in the bedroom reminded me of the permanence of the situation. Throwing myself back on *my* bed, I tried taking deep breaths. My chest was constricting and my head pounding. I could feel the panic attack creeping up on me.

"Lucy."

The sound of his voice did it. "I, I can't."

"Lucy, I don't want to fight."

"No!" Panting, I sat up and dropped my head between my legs. "Panic. Attack." I felt the bed dip under his weight and his hand began rubbing soothing circles across my back.

"I don't think I've seen you have an attack since we were kids."

"Not helping."

Once I was calm again, he told me to shower and that he'd order some dinner. I didn't want to fight either and did as he suggested. Walking out of the bedroom in sweats, I looked for him, but didn't see him. Someone knocked on the door and I froze, not sure what to do.

"Heath!" Another knock came. "Dammit." Looking through the peephole, I spotted a delivery guy. I opened the door as the young man handed me a large bag of food. It smelled like Chinese or Thai and my stomach grumbled in response.

"The money's on the counter." Heath's voice came from the direction of Will's room.

"Hang on." Setting the food on the counter, I found a couple twenties and snatched it up. Walking to the delivery buy, I inquired, "How much?"

"Twenty-two seventy-one." I handed him the two twenties and told him to keep the change. It wasn't my money and I figured Heath was feeling generous. "Thanks! Happy New Year."

"Same to you." Closing the door, I walked back to the kitchen and when I looked up, an Adonis was walking toward me in nothing but a towel. Bastard! Struggling the urge to stare at him, I tended to the food.

"Where's the change?"

"There wasn't any." I lifted my chin and gave him a big grin.

"Seriously. That's like an eighty percent tip."

Shrugging my shoulders, I quipped, "It's a holiday."

"So that's how it's going to be?"

Full of sarcasm, I retorted, "I don't know what you mean?" He grumbled under his breath as I asked, "Did you want to say that louder?"

"Nope."

Not sure where anything was kept, I started opening and shutting various cabinet doors and drawers. He stepped in my path and pulled out plates, setting them on the counter. He scooped some food on his plate, grabbed a fork, and sat down on the leather couch still wearing just a towel. *Really, dude?*

"You comfortable?" He met my eyes as I looked at his towel and then back to his eyes. Setting his plate down on the coffee table, I was relieved to think he was going to get dressed.

"Actually, no." Pulling the towel away and letting it drop to the floor, he sat back down. Grinning, he said, "That's better," and picked his plate back up.

Ok. Two could play that game. "You know, you're right. It's awfully hot in here." It totally wasn't, but I didn't care. I wiggled out of my sweats, taking my panties with me, and then pulled the hoodie over my head. Putting some food on my plate, I joined him on the couch knowing full-well he couldn't take his eyes off of me. Stabbing a piece of meat with my fork, I plopped it in my mouth, letting my teeth scrape against the metal.

I caught him staring at my tits and cleared my throat. He made no apologies and took a few bites of his food. I was still crazy pissed at him, but the sexual tension between us was palpable. I didn't want to think about the damage my wet pussy was causing to the leather couch and then I wondered how many other naked women had been on this couch. Disgusted, I stood and turned to walk away.

His arms caught around my waist and with a thud, I was on my back on the couch with him above me. "Where do you think you're going?"

He was nuzzling my neck and I wanted to resist him, but I couldn't. I wanted him with every fiber of my being. "Get off of me you pig."

"Oink, oink." I groaned and he smirked. He began kissing his way down my body and I caved, letting myself get lost in his touch. "I'm still angry with you."

"Join the club." He nipped at my nipple, sucking it into his mouth as I moaned. "We'll talk...later."

"Mmm. Promise."

"Promise."

My skin was sticking to the leather, increasing the temperature of the air around us. Running my fingers through the slick strands of his hair, I pushed his head lower. His arms circled under my thighs, spreading my legs further apart as he buried his face between them. So quickly he was able to get my body to react to him that I had to fight to keep control.

Fingers pumped in and out of me then he started twisting them, turning into my own personal vibrator.

"Heath!"

"CHRIST!" *That* wasn't Heath. My body stiffened, hands flying to hide my face, but I didn't dare open my eyes. "If we're going to live together there are going to be some fucking ground rules." Will was home. "Keep the fucking to the bedroom, would ya? I'll be in my room. Let me know when it's safe to come out." I heard his footsteps retreating and took note that I didn't hear any other steps. He was alone. "And clean off the couch, too!"

When the thud of his door slamming rang through the air, I opened my eyes. I found Heath just smiling at me, ready to pick up where Will had so rudely interrupted us. "Get off of me."

"Relax."

"HEATH! Get up!" I pried myself out from under him, my back peeling off the leather as I went. "What is wrong with you?" I jumped to my feet, picked up my clothes, and ran to the bedroom.

By the time Heath joined me there, I was dressed and curled up on the bed. "Are you hungry? You didn't eat much."

"Not really."

He sat down next to me and I saw that he wore lounge pants and a tank. "If you change your mind, it's in the fridge." He sighed and rubbed my hip, "It's not very late. Do you want to go out or watch a movie? It's New Year's Eve and all." I just shook my head. "I'm trying here, Lucy."

"I know. I'm just tired." I pulled myself to a seated position and decided, "A movie might be nice. Can we stay in here, though?"

Smiling, "Sure. That sounds great." He joined me on the bed and pulled me to his side as we scrolled the listings for something to watch.

~ CHAPTER 24 ~

~ HEATH ~

Our biggest fight since being married had happened
and we were still standing, for now. At least it was something
we were good at, besides the sex. Being so close to her was
making me crazy. Her scent, which still lingered on my lips,
and mere presence were intoxicating to me.

After Will caught us on the couch, me face down in her
pussy, I knew this living arrangement was going to get old real
fast. We were now cuddled in bed watching a movie, City of
Angels. I'd never really watched it until now, though the
theme song had been one of my favorites. Having her curled
into my side, I was thankful to really be seeing it for the first
time with her.

As the credits rolled and *Iris* by The Goo Goo Dolls
played, I rubbed her side. "Lucy?"

There was no response and I wondered how long she'd
been asleep. I couldn't see her face as she slept on my chest,
but I didn't dare move her either. I wanted to enjoy this
moment of peace. This was what I wanted with her, more

than anything, and it's what we'd been enjoying before she found out the truth on Christmas.

Rewinding the credits, I listened to the song again. It'd made it on one of the CDs I'd made her all those years ago. CDs that I found in her car on my drive to New York, after I left her and Will at the lake house. My mother was the only explanation.

I woke a few hours later with her still draped over my body. Looking to the clock, it was past 2 a.m.

"Happy New Year, Lucy." She didn't respond, didn't move, and so I dared to say what I'd been dying to say. "I love you. Always have, always will."

In the morning, I rolled over and found the bed empty. Panic set in as I leapt from the bed. Opening the bedroom door, I almost ran her down. She was carrying a tray of food and the glass of juice tipped over, soaking the pancakes.

"Dammit!"

"I'm sorry. It's my fault."

"I have more." She was headed back to the kitchen and I snatched the plate with the orange juice covered pancakes as she gave me a confused look. "Heath, I can make more."

Stuffing a soggy bite into my mouth, she grimaced at me. "Nope. I'll eat them."

"That's disgusting."

I just shrugged my shoulders and continued to eat them. "You're not eating?"

"I had some oatmeal."

I eyed her suspiciously and pointed at my plate, "Did you poison them?"

That smile I loved took over her face. "How long has it been?" She looked to the clock, "Poison should be kicking in any minute now."

I started to pretend I was choking and then fell to the floor as she stared on, not impressed. "Lu, Lucy. I'm choking."

"It's a pity I don't know the Heimlich. Should I call 9-1-1?" She stood over me and just smiled. "On second thought, do you have life insurance?"

"Yes."

Sighing, "Then I guess you're worth more dead than alive." She winked and moved a little closer with her hands resting on her hips.

"It's not that much money. You'll be sadly disappointed."

"I'm sure the gyms are worth money. I could sell your share, which would be mine once you're dead." I lurched up and grabbed her wrist, yanking her down to me. "Hey! It was a joke!"

"If I'm dying, I'm taking you with me!"

"How serial killer of you!" I began tickling her as we laid on the floor.

"Jesus Christ, you two. I thought we discussed this last night." Will. "Can't you keep it to the bedroom, or at least warn me? We can come up with a schedule if need be."

Lucy stood up, as she regained her breath.

"Chill out. Nothing was happening." She started cleaning up the dishes from breakfast and then pulled a plate from the microwave with another stack of pancakes. Offering them to Will, I complained, "What the hell? You had more the whole time and made me eat the orange juice covered ones?" She just shrugged her shoulders and smiled.

Will accepted and gave me a cheesy smile as he dug in to his breakfast. "This, this is ok. I could get use to this."

Lucy raised her brows and looked at both of us. "Don't get any ideas. I'm not his maid or chef and I won't be yours either." With that, she went back to the bedroom and slammed the door.

Will looked to me and noted, "Things seem good with you two."

"Eh. They could be better."

"They could be worse."

"Touché."

Walking to the bedroom, I heard the shower running and saw that the bathroom door was ajar. I took it as my invitation. Just as I walked in and began removing my pants, her voice filled the bathroom.

"Don't even think about it Heathcliff!"

I looked to the clear shower door, already covered in steam as her figure teased me. "You have five minutes and if you're not out, I'm joining you."

She cracked open the door and glared at me. She opened her mouth to say something and then groaned closing the door again. "I'll be out in a minute."

"Tick, tock."

When I walked back into the bathroom a few minutes later, I found her standing at the sink with a towel wrapped around her. She was running a comb through her wet strands and I walked past her, never taking her out of my peripheral vision. I turned the water back on and dropped my pants and underwear in one fluid movement.

I caught her arm still mid stroke through her hair, taking in my nakedness. When her eyes caught mine staring at her while she stared at me in the mirror she averted her eyes and began running the comb through her hair more roughly. I walked up behind her and placed my hands on her bare shoulders.

"See something you like?"

She scoffed, "It's nothing I haven't seen."

Smiling, I rebuffed, "That's not what I asked."

I dropped my lips to her exposed shoulder and began kissing and nipping at her skin. Feeling her body respond to my touch was one of the greatest rewards. A shiver ran up her spine as her body relaxed ever so slightly against mine. Her eyes had fluttered shut and the comb fell from her fingers. I don't even think she was aware of it until she pressed her lower back against the evidence of my desire for her.

"We have to stop." Her words were breathy and labored.

"Says who?" My arm circled around her and rested above her pounding heart.

"What?" She was dazed and trying to regain her bearings. "Says me!" Pulling her ear into my mouth, she moaned and her arms searched for something to hold on to.

"Let me take care of you. You need this as badly as I do." My breath came hot and heavy against her skin as she turned her head to give me better access. Pressing her ass into me, my hand moved to her hair and gripped a handful. I could feel her still fighting it, her body not fully under my control.

"I can't say no to you."

"Then say yes," I demanded.

"Oh, I, Heath." She was fighting herself, me, us and I understood, but I was going to try with all I had to get her to surrender. "You don't understand."

"I understand completely. I can't say no to you either."

Her body tensed as she pushed against me in rejection. "You left me!" My movements ceased as I met her eyes in the mirror. The minute my grip loosened on her, she turned to face me. "We still haven't talked."

I was a coward and walked away, climbing into the shower. "What's left to say?"

She flung open the shower door and questioned me. "Is that how you really feel, that there's nothing left to say?" Her eyes searched mine before I closed them and let the water wash over my face. "There's everything left to say." Her voice had become broken and soft, the fight in it gone.

"This is why this can't work. Not like this." Her eyes scrunched together and she shook her head at me. "All you women want to do is talk." I was being a jerk on purpose. Why did we have to talk when we both knew what our bodies wanted?

"Why are you being so callous? If you wanted a doormat, someone who'd let you fuck her anytime you want, you married the wrong girl. Where's the man I got to know on my honeymoon? The man who stayed up and talked all night getting to know me, because this man," she waved her finger at me, "this man is an asshole and I don't deserve it."

I didn't even know what to say to her. As she turned and walked away, my hand reached for her too late. Fucking and fighting is what we were good at and I didn't want to be fighting. I wanted to fuck. She wanted to talk.

We needed to talk and lay our cards on the table, but it terrified me. What if I wasn't what—who—she wanted? Part of me knew better. She was here, wasn't she? What was I so afraid of? I never talked emotions with any other woman. She was the closest I'd ever been to a woman, besides my mother. I knew one thing for sure. I loved Lucy and hated her all at once because I knew *she* was the one person who had the potential to destroy me. As long as I didn't destroy myself first.

I took too long in the shower, letting the water beat at my body as I let myself become numb. When I climbed out and made my way to the bedroom for clothes, she wasn't there. Once I dressed, I discovered she'd left the apartment too. *Shit!* I'd screwed it up all over again. Where could she have gone? Most places were closed since it was a holiday.

~ CHAPTER 25 ~

~ LUCY ~

That evening when I got home, having spent most of the day with Stacey, I found our apartment empty. *Our apartment.* Was it really ours or was it still his? I pushed the thought aside. Stacey urged me to go home and talk to him, not fully understanding that Heath didn't 'talk'. He charmed, fucked, and possessed my body, but rarely did he talk. No other man had ever been able to get my body to react—or should I say submit—the way Heath was capable of.

I fell asleep on the couch that night waiting for him. Will hadn't been around all day either and I vaguely wondered where he was. I debated about going to the gym, but didn't want to risk running into *her.* In a last ditch effort, I texted him as I lay on the couch under a blanket.

Please come home.

There was no response. I wasn't above begging, but I wasn't going to make a fool of myself either. I resumed the sound system which had his CDs playing on repeat. I'd found the CDs still in the front seat of my car—where I'd left them during the snowstorm—and wasn't even sure if Heath had noticed them. They meant more to me than I thought he'd ever know.

I cried myself to sleep that night and the next. Each morning I awoke in our bed, having been carried there by someone, but neither Heath nor Will were anywhere to be found. Our lives began this cycle of ships passing in the night. I'd go to bed alone and I'd wake in the morning alone, wondering if he'd really held me that night or if it'd just been a fleeting dream. This went on for longer than I cared to admit.

I kept my routine—grateful I had that to distract me—but had no idea what his routine was. We'd never really discussed it and now I wondered if he'd been a figment of my imagination. The only evidence of his existence were the dirty clothes piling up that he discarded in the hamper.

That evening, a couple weeks later, I ran into Will. It was all I could do to make eye contact and not break down. Will talked about O and his progress and let me know that Heath was spending all his spare time there. I guess I kind of assumed as much which is why I wasn't entirely frantic. I became horribly upset with myself because I had yet to go visit O.

"Do you think O would mind if I stopped in to see him?" Will nodded as guilt swept through me. "I should've gone to see him sooner, I just, I figured Heath would take me."

Will placed a hand on my shoulder and consoled me. "Go see O. He'd love to see you, especially since you're his sister now." He winked and headed to his bedroom.

The next day I headed to O's after work and walked up the flight of stairs to his apartment. As I climbed the stairs I immediately became sick to my stomach for O. He'd lost his leg and lived on the third floor in a building with no elevators. I took a few deep breaths before knocking on the door.

It took a minute, but when the door swung open I wasn't prepared for what I saw. Laughter and boisterous voices trickled out into the hallway where I stood. D'Artagnan stared back at me, a beer in his hand, as voices I didn't recognize infiltrated my senses.

"Who is it D?"

D looked at me and waved me in. As he did, he announced, "Our sister."

My eyes took in the scene and I was both happy, livid, and relieved. O sat at a table playing cards with Heath and some guys I didn't recognize. D took the empty seat as I bore my eyes into the back of Heath's skull. He hadn't even bothered to look at me.

I became distracted when I realized O was hobbling his way up, pulling his crutches up to support him, making his way toward me. He wrapped his free arm around me and hugged me. I clung to him, but not as long as I wanted. He was alive and smiling when in all reality he shouldn't have been.

O sensed the tension in me and tried to make a joke. "Come to bring your husband home? He could probably use the ride." He cupped his hand in the air and took a swig of the imaginary drink he held to let me know that Heath had been drinking.

I was pissed. While I'd been sitting at home worrying for him for over a week, he'd been here, with O, getting drunk? "I'm sorry. I wasn't aware I had a husband. If I had one I'd expect him to warm my bed at night and grace me with his presence occasionally."

O took a step back as I jumped at the sound of Heath's hands slamming down on the table. Heath stood and walked toward me as everyone else pretended to ignore the fight that was about to happen. Staring over their beers and cards in our direction, they waited along with me for what Heath would say and do.

Without waiting for my reply, gripping my forearm, he dragged me to the back of the apartment, bellowing, "Can I talk to you?"

Making sure everyone could hear, I bit out, "Sure, I wasn't aware talking was something you knew how to do."

He shoved me into a bedroom and slammed the door behind us. As I looked around the room I was well aware that it wasn't O's room. Items of Heaths were strewn across the room.

"So, are you living here now?"

"What the fuck are you talking about?"

I watched as he scrubbed his hands over his face before gliding them through his hair. My patience was growing thin. "You know you still haven't told me why you left. I had to find out about O from Will."

"I'm sorry."

I rolled my eyes at his lackluster apology, "Please. You are not." He moved past me and sat on the bed. I stood there with my arms crossed over my chest for far too long. After sighing, I headed for the door. "This is bullshit."

As my hand reached for the door I heard his broken voice beg me to stay. "Please don't go, Lucy. I need you." My heart broke a little at his plea. I closed my eyes, still facing the door, debating about what to do. "Will and I have been taking shifts, staying here, to make sure O's ok. Fuck. He's not ok." I turned to face him. His hands covered his face as he propped them on his knees.

"Heath?" His voice cracked as I looked closer at him. Was he crying?

"My brother is a better man than any of us. He doesn't deserve this. It should've been me. I should've gone with him."

I closed the space between us and got on my knees. Gently, I pulled his hands away and cupped his tear streaked face. "Heath, what happened to O isn't your fault. There's nothing you could've done." His eyes looked to my face and I could smell the liquor on his breath. "He seems to be in good spirits. Why didn't you tell me? I've been worried..."

"About what?"

"About you, us, O. Everything." There was something else I needed to talk to him about, too. "Heath, we only have four weeks left to decide if we're staying married."

Part of the terms of this whole experiment was to agree to eight weeks of marriage. At the end of eight weeks we had to decide if we were staying together or getting a divorce. It also meant that we'd been married for just over a month. A month anniversary that'd come and gone with no words of love from each other. I'd already dodged phone calls asking us to schedule our therapy appointments to see how things were going. I didn't even know if they knew that Heath had taken Will's place at the ceremony.

His eyes looked back and forth between mine and then traveled to my lips as I licked them. I should've known better than to get so close to him. Kneeling between his legs, all I wanted to do was to curl into his warmth. He was clearly hurting and distraught about O and his new circumstance. What I didn't know was if any of that hurt had to do with me or not?

He pulled on a lock of my hair that'd dropped in front of my eyes and twisted it around his fingers. "God, I've missed you."

Before I could respond, his mouth covered mine. His whiskers were a welcome feeling against my skin, but the alcohol was overpowering. I clung to his wrists as he cupped my face. His tongue lapped at my upper lip as I opened my mouth for him. He tasted like pretzels and booze, bitter and salty all at once and I wanted, no needed, more. My hands moved up his forearms, enjoying every curve of every muscle and tendon.

His arms moved down my body and yanked me onto the bed with him. His body hovered over mine, his hands frantically pulling my shirt up searching out my skin. Sucking on my neck, his hand was moving down my torso and was between my legs before I knew it.

"Lucy," he pressed his hand against my warmth and I closed my legs around it to keep him there, "I need you." His fingers worked over my scrubs, through my panties and had me nearly begging for more.

"I need you, too. I miss you, please come home. We can work this out, but I need you home."

"Take these off. I need to feel you, all of you." He pressed his cock against my thigh, like I needed the reminder of his current state.

"Heath, not here."

"Why not?"

"They could hear."

"So what?" He began pulling at my scrub pants as I tried pulling away.

"Heath, I said no. Not here. Please, take me home and I'll be all yours."

Slow and thick he whispered in my ear, "I want you to be all mine here and now."

There was a knock on the door and some obscene comment from someone I didn't recognize. I suddenly felt like I was back in college at some party and I didn't like it. I took the opening and wiggled out of Heath's grip, standing. As I pulled my shirt back down, Heath got up on his elbows and looked up at me.

"They're just messing around. Come back here."

Huffing, I gritted out. "Last chance to come home. Did you get my texts?"

He glared at me, silently challenging me. "Maybe I am home."

My mouth fell open and I knew he was drunk and I wasn't going to argue with a drunk man. I'd been there, done that. "You're drunk and still an asshole." I flung open the door and stopped. I didn't want to leave things this way so I made one last ditch effort. "Your home is with me. I'm not going anywhere, but I won't wait forever either, Heathcliff."

I marched out of the room and ignored the eyes staring at me as I walked out the front door. Slamming the door, the tears poured out of my eyes as I wrapped my arms around myself.

"Lucy?" Looking up I found Will walking up the stairs toward me. "What's wrong?"

What I said I didn't mean, but I couldn't stop myself from saying it either. "You should've just left me at the altar if you didn't want me. It would've been better!" He stared at me dumbfounded as I bit out, "Handing me to him…you just made everything worse."

"How did I make it worse?"

Instead of saying, 'Because now my heart's involved', I kept silent, pushing my way past him and left.

I couldn't think straight and thought for sure I was losing my shit. I didn't even know where to go. Home was the only option, but it just reminded me of him, us. Stacey was at work and Jaime had a new baby. I couldn't burden either of them. Cranking the volume, The Pretty Reckless was on. *You* drifted through the speakers with its soft acoustic sound. Didn't he want me, need me? Maybe not in the same way I needed him. He told me he wanted me, but *need* was another beast that could take you down a slippery slope of regret. *Need* was a big burden only few could take on.

I began to wonder if I'd ever been enough for him or if I ever would be. I couldn't deal with the possibilities of the answer to that question. Then it dawned on me and the tears came faster. Had he even been spending his nights at O's alone, his bed empty? Mistrust began to sink in and work its way through the cracks of my heart.

~ CHAPTER 26 ~

~ HEATH ~

Did she say she'd texted me? I'd never received a text. Absently, I searched for my phone in my pocket but didn't find it. Likely an excuse to try to make it look like she really gave a damn. If she did she'd know that I needed to get lost in her, her body, and the places we could go together. Once naked in each other's arms we had a way of transporting ourselves to a new level. At least that's how I felt.

A couple more days passed with no interaction. That night she'd come to O's, I hadn't made it back to the poker game. My head was pounding and I let sleep take me. I missed her, clearly, but O needed me. The only time I spent at the gym was when I had scheduled clients. I'd pop into the apartment when I knew she was at work or sleeping. More than once in those weeks, I'd found her asleep on the couch and I'd carry her to bed, holding her for a while before I'd leave again.

I was sitting on O's couch, staring off into space when his voice brought me back to reality. He'd been at a therapy appointment and D was bringing him home. I hadn't even heard the door open.

"Dude, what are you doing? Why are you still here? When are you going to fight for her?" I glared at O, taking offense but trying to reign my temper in. "So you're just going to let her push you away and call it a day?"

"You don't know anything about this, about us."

He dared to laugh. "The hell I don't. You love her, have since that summer and not ONCE have you fought for her. Not really."

He pulled up a chair and sat down in front of me—the space empty where his lower left leg should've been jutting out between us—he got nose to nose with me and poked me in the chest.

"Back off, O."

"She needs you to prove to her that she's worth the fight." He grabbed my shirt and shook me. "Fight. For. Her." Then he released me causing my back to thump against the back of the couch. "What I wouldn't give to have a love like hers."

Standing again with the help of his crutches, he turned toward the hallway and I thought for sure he would leave without another word. Talking to the wall, I knew his words were meant for me. "You're so damn stubborn, always have been. I've watched you go through losing her without a fight. I won't do it again. Not like this. Will isn't the only one who knows your secrets." Then he left the room, making his way back to his bedroom.

I sat there for close to thirty minutes before I made my way to the spare bedroom and packed my bag. He was right, though I'd never admit that to him. I needed to go home and fight for her.

When I pulled into the parking lot, her car was there. I took a deep breath before heading up, not sure what to expect from her. Going directly upstairs, I found the apartment barren. Neither Will nor Lucy anywhere to be found, both probably at work. Sighing in resignation, I changed my clothes and headed downstairs. I'd neglected work long enough.

Finding a pile of bills and invoices to sort through once in the gym office, I got to work. I'd been working for several hours when a pair of feminine hands began massaging my neck. Not even thinking for one minute about who it was and the consequences that could follow, I let myself enjoy it.

Before I knew it, she was whispering in my ear. "She isn't taking care of you the way I could."

Alarms went off in my head as I stood up and turned on Stella. "This has to stop, Stella. She's my wife and I don't plan on changing that." She tilted her head at me and came closer, smiling that siren smile of hers. "What happened between us was strictly casual. You know that."

"It was more than casual and pretty damn recent. I wonder if Lucy knows how recent?"

"Don't you threaten me, Stella." I was angry, but trying to keep my voice down.

She poked me in the chest, "Don't *you* threaten me! I can make Montrose disappear with the snap of my fingers. Lucy, too."

She was playing with fire, but I wasn't sure if she was bluffing or not. We'd signed papers for the Montrose gym, but she didn't know that. I'd slept with her, more recent than I cared to remember, but I was single when it happened and it was a mistake. I'd told her that after it happened.

"Lucy knows, so save your breath." Lucy knew there was something, but I hadn't been exactly truthful about when it'd ended with Stella. Shit. Stella still thought it was going on.

I grabbed my phone and stood. Stella closed the distance between us as I backed up against the desk, her cleavage against my chest. There was a knock on the office door. I had to get away from Stella before it just got worse. After the knock, the door swung open and I was met with Lucy. I didn't try pushing Stella off of me. Lucy saw it all and there was nothing I could do about it.

"Hey Lucy. We were just talking about you."

"Stella!"

With a smile on her face, she brushed past me making sure her cleavage rubbed against my arm. "Toot-a-loo."

My head was instantly pounding. Lucy was looking at me, but her eyes weren't focused on me. Almost like she was staring through me. Her hands were clenched into fists at her side. I closed my eyes and took a deep breath.

My imagination got away with me as I envisioned a cat fight. Lucy slamming Stella's over inflated head through the wall seemed like an appropriate thing about now and the thought had me smiling. She had said she'd 'cut a bitch', or was it shank?

"Lu…" I opened my eyes and she was gone. "What the fuck?"

Frantically, I turned the lights off and locked the office door and ran after her. Assuming she headed for the apartment, I heard the door slam as I climbed the stairs after her. Upon opening the door, I then heard our bedroom door slam as I made my way into the apartment.

Here we go.

I walked in and found her sitting on the edge of the bed. Cautiously, I walked to where she was sitting and sat down next to her. "Nothing happened. She's trying to get you worked up."

"If you don't get rid of her, I will."

I half chuckled, not sure if she was serious or not. "Excuse me?"

"You heard me." We sat in silence as I digested her words. Stella had to go, I agreed, but she posed a threat if I

- 224 -

fired her. I had to bide my time until Montrose was set in stone.

"It's complicated, Lucy. She handles all the office stuff."

"So find someone new."

Sighing. My eyes began searching the room as I thought about what to do. Lucy was right. "Ok. She's gone."

Her head darted toward me as she hesitated, "Really?"

Nodding, I confirmed, "Really. It's been a long time coming. I'll talk to Will. We'll figure it out."

She leaned into me slightly and pulled back just as quick. "Thank you."

"You're welcome. I should've done it ages ago. Give me some time to try to find a replacement."

"Oh, ok." We sat in silence before she asked, "Is there something I can help with? I'm pretty good with numbers."

Smiling, I looked at her and added, "Don't tease me."

"Who said I was teasing? I worked for my brother and Dorian when I wasn't in school. I can help." I studied her and knew the minute she started to wonder if I believed her truly capable. "Or not."

"No." Her eyes scrunched, "No, I mean yes. Your help would be great. When do you want to start?"

Pushing out a breath, she smiled, "I can start now, if you want."

I kissed her cheek and took her hands in mine. "You sure you want to work alongside Will and I?"

"I'm not quitting my job Heath. But I'll help out where I can."

"Right."

"Heath. We need to talk."

Exhaling, I agreed. "I know."

"They want to see us. We were supposed to have a session two weeks ago to check our progress."

The therapists were the last people I wanted to see, but I also wanted this to work. "Tell me when and where. I'll be there."

"Ok. I'll call them tomorrow to make the appointment."

The next afternoon Lucy left me a note that we were meeting with the therapists that night at six. She had to work and said she'd meet me there. I talked to Will and he agreed to let Stella go, but we had to find a replacement first. We moved mine and her schedules around so we were rarely in the gym together. It was the best we could do for now.

I met Lucy in the lobby that night just as they called us back. Dr. Phillips appeared to be the only one in the session. We took a seat and I stretched my arm on the back of the sofa behind Lucy.

"So. We haven't spoken since before the ceremony. Tell me how things are?" We both hesitated as Dr. Phillips looked back and forth between both of us. "What's the problem?"

Lucy just spit it out. I knew it'd come up, but she just dove right into it. "Will was my match and Heath, his twin brother, took his place."

Dr. Phillips was clearly shocked. "I'm sorry. What did you say?" Lucy began to speak and I stopped her and spilled it all to Dr. Phillips. Once I was done she began flipping through the file she held, frantically. "Hang on." She stood and got on her desk phone. "Can you bring me William Kerrigan's file? Yes, now!"

"That's not necessary."

Dr. Phillips head snapped to me and said, "Oh, yes indeed it is. Do you realize what you've done?" She looked to Lucy, "My dear, I'm so sorry."

Lucy was shaking her head, "I think you misunderstood. I'm glad Heath stepped in. I mean, it never would've worked with Will. I'm like a sister to him. And as much as I try to fight it," she grabbed my hand, "there's something here with Heath and I."

Relief flooded me as I squeezed her fingers between mine. Dr. Phillips dropped to her chair just as the receptionist stepped into the room and handed her a file and left just as quick.

"So, but," she started thumbing through both files, "I'm confused. The files are joined, yours and Heaths. But Will got the call?" We both nodded. It was as if she was talking to herself, "I don't understand." She put the files down and observed us.

"Wait." I needed a minute to catch up on everything she'd said. "So *you're* saying that Lucy and I *are* a match. Not Lucy and Will?"

"I need to dig into this deeper, but according to these files, yes. You're our first set of identical twins to go through the process. Now, if someone mixed up paperwork. I really don't know what to say. If someone made a mistake, I'll find out and we'll remedy this any way we can."

The hell she would. What did she expect me to do? Giving up my wife wasn't going to happen. "The hell you will." She looked to me and I wasn't sure what to say to get my meaning across.

"Heath, why did you feel it necessary to keep the truth from Lucy anyway?"

~ CHAPTER 27 ~

~ LUCY ~

I grew uncomfortable for Heath. I knew why he'd lied. He was still convinced I'd pick Will over him and maybe he was right to believe that. There had been so much animosity between us over the years that it'd be the easy assumption for anyone to make.

I interrupted Heath before he could say too much. "Dr. Phillips. Heath lied because of me. We have a history and I was never honest about how I felt about him, causing him to doubt himself." Heath stared at me, almost dumbfounded.

"So, do you want me to look into this further, find out if paperwork was mixed up or not?"

I looked into Heath's eyes and he spoke before I could. "I want to know."

"Heath? I think we should move forward and let it go."

"Lucy, I believe that you're my match, but I can't carry on wondering if I was the one who was supposed to get that call. I need to know that it was more than intuition on my part."

I studied his eyes and understood why he needed to know. But it scared me to death, too. What would he do if he found out what we assumed all along? He wasn't my match and Will was. Would it change things? He'd married me assuming that and I didn't think it needed to be said again. But, if there was some kind of mix up and he *was* really my match, it would bring us both relief.

"Ok."

"This is what we'll do. I want you two to go out and have some fun. Unless I'm wrong, there's great chemistry between you two." I felt myself blush and she smiled. "Enjoy each other as husband and wife. It's clear that you both care deeply for one another and it's the first time a couple of ours has had such an intricate history. I'll call you when I get some answers and we can schedule another session. You only have a few weeks left before you need to make a decision." She smiled and stood. "Sound good?"

We both agreed. I felt closer to Heath than I had since the supposed truth was revealed Christmas night. Now it all seemed for naught; his 'lie' and my reaction to it all. There was a good chance that Heath *had* been my match all along. It was easy to believe that they had called Will by mistake given the twin thing. Their files were probably kept right next to one another. That was my reason and I was sticking to it.

When we made it to the parking lot, he walked me to my car. "You want to grab some dinner?" He seemed lost in thought and I stroked his face. "Heath? Are you ok?"

His eyes traveled to mine and he shrugged his shoulders. "I'm ok."

"Please don't worry about the possible mix-up. I want us to move on, away from all this craziness." He still seemed solemn so I took a chance. Getting on the balls of my feet, I pressed my lips to his. "Come back to me." His mouth opened to mine and soon his hands were in my hair. I clutched to him and soon pulled my lips from his, trying to catch my breath. "Take me home, Heath." My hand traveled to his waist and palmed his erection as I whispered, "I want to taste your Heath bar."

His groan traveled through my body like a bolt of electricity. "Don't tease me, Lucy."

Wrapping my hand around him as best I could through his jeans, I moaned, "I'm not teasing. I've missed you. I just want to get lost in you."

Reaching behind me, he opened my car door and nearly pushed me in my seat. "Get your ass home. I'll meet you there."

I chuckled as he leaned over me and helped me buckle. "Whoever gets home last comes last." His eyes searched mine and then got my meaning.

"You're going down."

"Not until you go down on me." I closed my door and threw it into reverse as he hurried to his car. I ran every yellow light I could get away with and was several minutes ahead of him, I hoped, by the time I pulled into the parking lot behind the gym.

I ran upstairs and rushed to the kitchen grabbing a bottle of wine. I kicked my shoes off as I set the bottle down on the dresser. Shit! I needed a corkscrew. I ran back to the kitchen as the front door flung open.

"Ha! You're too late, I beat you!"

"You could've been killed running all those lights."

I just smirked, "Give me five minutes."

"Whatcha got there?" I gripped the corkscrew tighter behind my back as he lifted his chin. "You have two minutes."

Backing through the bedroom door, I closed it and threw my clothes off. I didn't bother leaving a stitch of clothing on. I pulled up my music list and hit play on my phone. Pulling the tie from my hair, I let it fall around my shoulders. I quickly pulled the cork free from the bottle and sat on the bed, with the bottle between my legs, just as the door opened.

His eyes traveled over my body as he stepped into the room, closing the door behind him. *Line of Fire* by The Veronicas was playing as he stepped in closer. He began undressing and I watched with eager eyes.

I took a swig of the wine and then let a good amount dribble over my body as I leaned back. His hooded eyes watched as the wine flowed into my belly button and down over my pussy.

"Dinner's served."

He dropped to his knees in front of me and yanked my ass to the edge of the bed. "Exactly what I was hungry for, too." His tongue dipped into my navel, licking any remnants of the wine away. I poured more on as he bit on my hip.

He crawled over me and I had no choice but to lay flat on the bed. Taking the bottle from my hands, he took a swig and then another. Lifting the bottle to my lips, he gave me a drink before pouring more down my neck and then set the bottle down. His mouth licked every inch of my neck and across the top of my chest. My fingers clawed at his shoulders before reaching between us. Squeezing his cock, he sucked in a sharp breath.

"Fuck. I've missed you."

"Me too." Panting and clawing at his back, I tried pulling him closer. "Please, kiss me, Heath."

"We made a deal. I have to go down on you first."

Groaning, I pleaded, "Well hurry up then."

He chuckled as he moved down my body. When his tongue ran over my clit I thought I might die. My mouth became dry as I panted and moaned at his prowess. It wasn't long before I was on the verge of coming.

"Wait, stop." He lifted his head. "I want you inside of me when I come."

Wiggling his fingers, he said, "I am inside you."

Smiling, I panted, "You know what I mean. Please."
He hummed on my clit, "Shit, don't stop."

Lifting his head he asked, "Which is it?"

"Heathcliff!"

He motioned me to scoot up the bed and I did his
bidding. He seemed to be contemplating how he wanted me
when he sat down on the bed, legs stretched out in front of
him. "Come here." He patted his lap and I got up on my
knees and moved closer to him, having a hard time taking my
eyes off his cock that stood at attention.

His hands cupped my ass and pulled me close. Lifting
one leg over his, he pressed his thigh into my crotch, eliciting
a moan from me. His mouth moved between my breasts as
his hands kneaded the back of my thighs. Lowering his leg,
he reached behind and between my legs, easily gliding over
the slickness that covered me.

I lifted my other leg and straddled his lap. I stroked his
cock and guided him to my entrance. Moving him in small
circles against me, I took pleasure in the heat of his head
against my clit. He took control and slid his tip inside as I
grabbed his shoulders to steady myself.

"Heath." He sank in further as I tried slowing him. It'd
been long enough that I needed a moment to adjust to his
size. Pulling down hard on my shoulders, he sank into me
fully. I cried out in both pleasure and in pain.

"Did I hurt you?"

Wrapping my arms around his neck, "No, just give me a second."

"You're already throbbing around me, Lucy. I've missed your beautiful pink pussy."

I started to speak but couldn't muster any words as his hands lifted my ass and plunged into me again. "Jesus."

Though I didn't think he could hit me any deeper, I wanted to find out. I circled my legs around him and leaned back, searching for his mouth. My fingers ran over his obliques and down the rest of his torso. I loved his body and would never get enough of it. Gripping at his chest, we kissed in a frenzy. My hands reached around to his now damp back.

"I want to see you." Opening my eyes and leaning back, I rode him with my hands stretched out behind me. "Fuck, you're beautiful."

His hands held me as he yanked me on and off his cock with ease, driving me closer and closer to the brink. My arms were growing tired and like he sensed it, he pushed me back. My shoulders and head now on the bed as he sat up and fucked me. I happily handed all control over to him.

Panting, "I love you like this. Melting into the mattress and into me. I want to fuck you harder and harder just to make you crazy." I just nodded and cried out as he gave me even more. I'd be sore and smiled at the thought of it. "Touch yourself. Let's make you come undone."

Licking my fingers, I began circling my clit as he growled out. The pressure was building as I squeezed around him, my clit swelling even more. "Heath, oh, it feels so good."

"Fuck, you're going to push me out you keep squeezing so hard."

I smiled and tried to relax. A few moments later, one more lick of my fingers and I was circling my clit to my demise. "Heath, now! Please don't stop."

Knowing I needed him to keep fucking me, he pumped in and out with determination. He ended up on top of me, my hand pinned between our bodies as I slowed the circles around my tender nub. His mouth sucked on my neck as my body shook and jerked with satisfaction and then his body stiffened as he flooded into me. My free hand held him close as the hand between us turned to rub the root of his cock.

"Lucy. Sweet Lucy." He lifted slightly so I could pull my hand free. When I did he circled my wrist and held it above my head against the bed. I pulsed around him as he winced with pleasure. "Minx."

Rolling to his back, he pulled me with him where I fell asleep soon after.

~ CHAPTER 28 ~

~ HEATH ~

I woke up to her hands and lips scouring my body. It didn't take long for me to fully wake in every sense of the word.

Before she took me in her mouth, she smiled at me and said, "It's my turn."

Her warm mouth sheathed me as I watched her. "Lucy. Don't stop."

Her mouth made a popping sound as she released me, "Not a chance. My new favorite flavor."

The next few days went really well. Almost like all the bad that had happened never existed. When she wasn't working she was helping me at the gym. She was right and she did have a good feel for numbers. She started finding little errors here and there and began reconciling them for us.

I could picture her and I running the gyms together, at least this one, but I would never ask her to leave her profession. I rarely heard her complain about being a dental hygienist and I wasn't going to push her. Will and I really needed to find someone permanent. Until then, Lucy was our best bet.

The next day Will and I had another lunch meeting with Jameson. We were both annoyed, but kept our cool when Stella walked in. Jameson was on wife number three and Stella was the daughter of his second wife.

As Stella said hello to Jameson, Will asked me discreetly, "How'd she know about this meeting?"

I just shook my head. I had no idea, but I knew it wasn't just a coincidence.

"Please, join us Stella." Jameson motioned to the empty chair across from me and she shook her head. "Come on. A lovely lady like yourself." He looked to Will and I, "You don't mind do you, boys?"

Will asked her to join us as I took a deep breath and avoided making eye contact with her. We were almost done with the meal and Stella actually behaved herself. Will and I needed to discuss business, but we weren't comfortable doing so with her there.

Will was growing impatient and announced, "We don't want to keep you from your afternoon, Stella. We have business to discuss with Jameson if you have other things to attend to."

"Oh, not at all. Actually, I find the business side of things very interesting." She smiled before taking a sip of water as Will gripped his napkin in annoyance.

"Stella, can I talk to you in private?" I seized the moment knowing she couldn't resist a moment alone with me. I stood and when she nodded her approval, I pulled her chair out as we headed to the bar. Will was the businessman, I was just the muscle so to speak. I hoped taking Stella to the bar would give him enough time to schmooze with Jameson.

"Aren't you going to buy me a drink?"

Grunting, "Sure. Whatever you like." She waved down the bartender and ordered a Cosmo. She asked if I wanted anything and I responded, "Nope." As the bartender walked away I got to the point. "Cut the shit. What are you doing here?"

She pressed her lips together smugly and denied any wrongdoing. "Pure coincidence."

"So you just happened to be coming to this restaurant, alone, for lunch." She nodded her head. "Bullshit."

"Think what you want." The bartender dropped off her drink as I handed over some cash to cover it. "You don't really think I planned this do you?" She took a sip and I knew damn well she had. I just couldn't figure out why.

We sat there for a few minutes as I kept idle conversation with her while keeping an eye on Jameson and

Will. I spotted them both stand several minutes later and shake hands. Will made his way toward me.

"We're all set." He seemed to understand the question in my eyes and just nodded. "Jameson would like to see you, Stella." She seemed surprised to hear that and I was too. "Oh, and one more thing, Stella." She smiled, neither of us prepared for what Will would say. "You're fired." What the hell had Will done? Looking to me he huffed, "Let's go."

When we were out of earshot, I asked, "I thought we were waiting to fire her? Everything good? Should we be leaving them alone?"

"Chill out, it's all good. I filled Jameson in on her little obsession with you."

"You what?"

"No worries. He said he's used to her games. Montrose is ours."

I stopped him and he smiled. "What did you say?"

"It's ours."

I clenched my fists and threw them in the air. We hugged briefly. Opening a gym had been our dream and now we had a chain. I wanted to celebrate and there was only one person I wanted to do that with.

Will dropped me off at the gym and I immediately hopped in my car and ran to the store. I was going to cook her dinner and picked up some food and flowers before heading back home.

The pasta had just finished cooking when she walked in the door that night. The table was set and she smiled at me when she realized I'd cooked dinner. She walked over to me and got up on her tip toes to kiss me. Slinking my arms around her waist I pulled her closer.

Nuzzling into my chest, she asked, "Are we celebrating?"

"We are."

"What's the occasion?"

"Don't worry about that. Why don't you go get comfortable and I'll finish this." She pursed her lips, wondering what I was up to and nodded before heading to the bedroom.

As I finished fixing our plates and pouring the wine, she came out of the bedroom in a robe. I wasn't sure if she wore anything underneath and she knew what I was thinking.

My hands reached for her as she dodged them. "Ahh, nope. I'm eating my dinner first. It smells too good to pass up." I kissed her temple after she sat and then sat down across from her.

"We got Montrose."

Her eyes got big as she squealed. "Really?" I nodded as she leapt from her seat and sat in my lap. "Honey, that's great. I'm so happy for you."

Wrapping my arms around her waist, I kissed her as she cupped my face. I liked hearing her call me 'Honey'. "Thank you. It's pretty exciting."

"I'm so proud of everything you've accomplished. It's amazing."

"It's no biggie. I'd never be where I'm at without Will…and you." She tilted her head and mentioned something about having nothing to do with my success. I corrected her. "You're wrong, Lucy. I did this for you. Whether you realize it or not, or if I even realized it…But I wanted something to show for, to prove I was worthy."

"Heath, you've always been worthy." I wasn't sure how to respond. There were so many things I wanted to tell her, ask her. "What is it? You have that look on your face like you want to say something, but you're not sure if you should."

Smirking, I caved and asked her what I'd I wanted to since our session with Dr. Phillips. "What did you mean when you told Dr. Phillips that you hadn't been honest about your feelings for me?" She tried to hide her reaction, but she stiffened for a split second and then looked away from me. "Never mind. I don't want to push you." I felt guilty and insecure again and hated the power she had over me.

"You're not pushing." She took a deep breath. This couldn't be good. "I've been thinking about it, too. I think after that summer," she looked in my eyes to make sure I knew which one she was referring to and continued, "I latched on to my anger so tightly that I didn't know how to let go of it. I think if I'd figured out a way to let go of it I would've discovered something else entirely."

Narrowing my eyes, I asked, "Discovered what?"

She was playing with the sash on her robe, keeping her hands busy. It was a nervous habit of hers. "Love." She made eye contact and looked away, mistaking my look of shock for something else. She tried covering her tracks and mumbled, "Or deep like."

"Look at me." When she did I asked her to explain. "Tell me more."

"I just mean, I think that I was falling for you and deep down that scared me." Her voice quieted as she confessed, "It still scares me."

My heart was full and I wanted to tell her how I felt, with her awake and looking at me, but I wanted to hear her say it first. It was the last piece of armor I had against her and I refused to drop it until she said those three words first. Then I'd know I had her.

"Are you trying to tell me that you're falling for me?" When her eyes met mine, she took in my smile and pinched her lips together, her eyes grinning back at me.

"I think we both know that I fell for you long ago. I'm just finally admitting it."

Leaning my forehead against hers, I confided in her, "I fell for you long ago, too."

"Pinky swear?" She lifted her hand and held out her pinky to me.

Wrapping my pinky around hers, I agreed, "Pinky promise. Our little secret."

~ CHAPTER 29 ~

~ LUCY ~

It was the day of our meeting with Dr. Phillips and the day we had to make our decision on whether we were staying married or getting a divorce. I knew what my answer was without a doubt and I was pretty confident that Heath's answer was the same. We had yet to say those three little words, but I planned to tell him after our meeting.

The day was dragging at work and I couldn't wait to get the day over with. My last patient canceled so I drove home early. I ran upstairs when I didn't see his car in the parking lot. We'd agreed to meet at Dr. Phillips' office and he was probably visiting O and I didn't want to bother him. I pulled my scrubs off and put on a dress. It felt appropriate considering what we were embarking on.

It took every ounce of my willpower not to call or text him. The anticipation was killing me, but I also enjoyed the rush of it all. I headed to the therapy session and when I pulled into the parking lot, I looked for his car. It wasn't there so I waited for a few minutes before walking to the office. I didn't want Dr. Phillips to think we were late.

I sat in her waiting area for a few minutes and Heath still hadn't arrived. She popped her head out of her office and called me back.

"Heath's not here yet. Let me call him."

"It's ok. That just gives us some time to chat first." She smiled and I slipped my phone back in my purse and followed her into her office.

Once we were both seated she asked how things were and I replied, "Good. They're really good."

Like she knew I was holding back, she asked, "And?"

"I'm in love."

"Have you told him?"

"Not yet. I think we're both waiting for the other to say it first."

"If you truly believe that, maybe you should tell him. Some men can be very guarded using those three words. It's like their armor is gone once they reveal it." I smiled and agreed. I'd tell him the first chance we were alone.

She asked if I'd heard from him yet and I checked my phone. "This isn't like him."

"It's ok. So, I have the results." That caught my attention and I watched her pull a manila envelope to her lap. "You look scared."

I sighed and released a heavy breath. "I'm not sure I want to know. I don't have any regrets and he's who I want." Pointing at the envelope, "That won't change anything for me..."

"But?"

"I worry it has the potential to really hurt him."

"What if it's good news?"

I didn't respond. Just shrugged my shoulders. I wasn't sure the 50/50 odds were worth the risk to his pride. I wanted him, not his brother or anyone else and the results wouldn't sway that for me. If he wasn't my match on paper, I feared it had the potential to ruin him which could in turn ruin us.

Twenty minutes passed and I was growing worried. I kept checking my phone. He wasn't answering my calls or texts. Eventually our appointment came and went. I was growing livid.

"Lucy, listen. Let's not jump to conclusions. I just hope he's ok. We can reschedule, or not. Here," she handed me the sealed envelope, "open it together, or don't." We exchanged a brief hug and then I left.

When I got in my car I decided to call the gym. The receptionist said that Heath had left his phone at the gym, but he'd left me a message. I thought it a little strange, but didn't think anything of it. She gave me the name of a hotel and told me to check in at the front desk.

Driving to the hotel I was growing excited. I was still pissed he missed the meeting, but maybe he had this romantic evening planned. I couldn't wait to see what he had up his sleeve.

I stopped at the desk and was handed an envelope with my name on it. Inside was a key and the room number. My heart was racing as images of a rose petal covered hotel room danced through my mind. The elevator opened up to the designated floor. I walked the long hall, almost wondering if I was going the right way when I came upon a double door with the room number displayed.

Opening the door, a suite was revealed to me. Champagne and two glasses sat on the kitchenette and I could hear the water running. When I looked toward the bathroom, Heath walked out and he appeared angry. A towel around his waist, he stopped dead in his tracks when he saw me.

"Lucy. Let me explain."

Why was he so off kilter? "Explain what? I forgive you for missing the appointment with Dr. Phillips. This is so wonderful."

"Lucy, stop! Listen to me."

Apprehension set in as a figure flashed in front of me. Stella in a robe with wet hair. Looking to Heath, his hair was wet too. Every filter I had, left me and I became someone I didn't recognize. Someone only he pulled out of me. He was here with *HER* while I sat at an appointment where we were supposed to decide together whether we were to stay married or not.

"You son of a bitch!" He took a step toward me, spouting some excuse. *She* just smiled and sat down, enjoying the show. "You're a fucking skank." She tried to say something and I held up my hand to stop her. "You're messing with a marriage, MY marriage."

"Lucy."

I snapped at him, "I'm not talking to YOU." Glaring back at Stella I announced, "What we have goes deeper than anything you can imagine."

"Please. You've been married a couple months and only met the day you married. He…"

Cutting her off and smiling, I goaded her. "Is that so? Let me guess. You think you have some connection that will surpass time?" She tilted her chin up before I let her in on the secret I was now confident she didn't know. "What we have spans back decades." Her eyes narrowed in confusion. "It runs deeper than you could ever dream."

My pride stopped me from saying anything more as I realized I was defending my love—our love—to the slutbag trying to destroy it. And I couldn't get started on my douchebag husband. I turned and walked back out the door.

His arm came down around my wrist as he begged, "Let me explain. She did this. It's a trick."

Turning on him, I ripped my arm from his grip and spit out, "You really expect me to fucking believe that pile of shit? We had an appointment with Dr. Phillips tonight. If you didn't want to stay married, all you had to do was say so." Motioning to the room, "But this, this is just, just…"

"Just bullshit. Nothing happened. Please." He started rambling. "I forgot my phone at the gym. I called Cindy from O's and had her check it. She said you called and said the appointment was cancelled and to meet you here. I got my room key and came up here. I decided to hop in the shower and then, SHIT!"

"You're unbelievable and a horrible liar. Just admit it. Own it you bastard."

"Lucy, please. If ever there was a time for you to believe me, it's now. You just defended me to her, but you refuse to hear me out?"

"I'll always defend you. That doesn't mean I'm right to do so."

I stood and studied his eyes. Lying and honest, I couldn't tell the difference. He was Heath and he had my trust, honor, and love. But the proof was standing in front of me. He was in a towel, wet from the shower and Stella the same. He just stood there, silent and I took that as an admission of guilt.

"The results are in." He shook his head at me, not sure where I was going. I lied and decided to hurt him, maybe worse, than the way he'd hurt me. "There was no mix-up. Will's my match, not you."

"I, no. I don't believe you."

"Believe it. I'll let Dr. Phillips know that we're NOT staying married. You're not worthy."

Turning on my heels, I headed toward the elevator. When I made it to the silver double doors, my heart broke realizing he hadn't come after me. I needed to get to my car. I had to keep it together until then. I couldn't get the look on his face out of my head. His reaction was what I wanted and I felt horrible for it. Seeing Stella there, all I saw was red and words were my weapon.

Once I walked outside, the cold night air assailed me. As I made it to my car I realized I was going to be sick. Leaning in the bushes, I heaved the little bit of contents of my stomach. When I was finished, I got in my car. My words replayed in my head.

"Will's my match."

"You're not worthy."

The words cut me and my chest constricted at the thought of losing him. What had happened? What had I done? What had he done? Telling him he wasn't my match and that he was unworthy was adding insult to injury. The emotions overcame me and a guttural moan escaped my throat as I tried to catch my breath. Breathing, it hurt to do so. Dropping my head to my shaking arms, which rested like teetering pinnacles on my knees, I closed my eyes and feared that I'd lost him. Forever.

I started to head home which I knew couldn't be my home any longer. I tried calling Stacey and Jaime, neither answered. Getting on the freeway, I headed to the only other place I could think of.

O opened the door to his apartment and I burst into tears. He was my friend, like a brother, was my brother in marriage…for now. We had always been close and had spent a lot of time together these past few weeks since he'd been home. Once I thought about it, I knew this wasn't my best decision. Heath would easily find me here. Maybe that's what I wanted.

The next morning I woke in O's guest room. Heated voices were coming from the living room and I wasn't sure if it was Will or Heath, but the other voice was definitely O. I'd told him everything the night before and while he believed me, he was hesitant to believe Heath had cheated on me. I walked out of the room, still in my dress and found Will and O arguing.

"He's not coming here. Not while she's here. She needs space and I'm going to honor that."

"He's your brother. You should've stayed out of this."

"The way you are?"

"You guys. Stop." They turned to me and I agreed with Will. "Will's right, O. I shouldn't have come here."

Will looked at me and said, "I don't know what the fuck happened, but Heath is a wreck. What did you do?"

My blood was instantly boiling. "What did I do? Fuck you!"

"Will! You should be asking Heath what HE did." Will looked to O and then back to me.

I grabbed my purse and shoes and headed for the door. "I shouldn't be here."

"Whoa, whoa, Lucy, hang on. What's going on?"

I told him about what I found at the hotel, how he'd missed our appointment. "All I ever wanted was for this to work, with him. Finding him in that room, with her, both of them…" I couldn't even finish saying it. Sniffling and struggling to breathe I confessed, "I love him. I fell in love with him. And it's your fault. This never would've happened if you'd faced me at the altar or stood me up."

"What are you talking about?"

Not hearing his question I said, "He's broken my heart, again."

"Lucy, I don't know what you think you saw, but it's not. He wouldn't… Not with her. She's behind this somehow."

"It doesn't matter. If he wants it to be over, then it's over." I walked away from them and out the door as the tears tried blocking my vision with Will yelling after me.

"Lucy!"

~ CHAPTER 30 ~

~ LUCY ~

I drove around for what felt like hours listening to the CDs he'd made me and other songs that ripped at my heart. *Just A Little Bit Of Your Heart* by Ariana Grande was one that I played over and over again. Hesitantly, I pulled into the parking lot behind the gym. His car wasn't there. He was probably still at the hotel with *her*. It was better that way. I needed to get my things and go before he returned. Stacey or Jaime would take me in.

I wanted to believe Will; that Stella was behind everything, but how? She'd been fired and was out of the picture. Was it all a cover? If Heath thought he could have us both he was sorely mistaken. For a brief moment of insecurity, I believed that I could handle him having a mistress, if it meant I still had part of him. What the hell was wrong with me? I was losing it.

I was in our bedroom and staring at the bed as memories flooded me. Had I known that our last time together would be our last, I would've stayed awake all night worshiping his body as he worshipped mine. I grabbed a bag from the closet and walked to the dresser. My hands were shaking as I tried to pull the drawers open. How had I missed this, that whatever he had with Stella was more than a passing fling?

"Lucy!" The door bounced off the wall as he flung it open. "What are you doing? I've been looking for you everywhere." I couldn't bear to look at him. "Stacey and Jaime are worried. Where's your phone?"

I vaguely recalled throwing it at O's place after the battery died. "Phone's dead."

"Lucy. Please, you have to listen to me."

"Where were you all night?"

"Looking for you." He stepped closer and I moved further away. "I didn't think you'd run to O. Shit, I drove up to the lake house thinking for sure that's where you'd be."

"I think that I thought O's would be the first place you'd look for me."

"We still have so much to learn about each other."

"It's too late for that."

"I'm telling you right now. Nothing happened with Stella."

Waving him off, I screamed at him. "How could you miss our appointment? We talked about it all week."

"I told you, I called the office and Cindy told me that you canceled it." As if he was talking to himself, he said, "She

- 255 -

must know something." Picking me up off the floor, I tried fighting him off. "Come on."

"Let go of me."

"Not until we talk to Cindy."

Dragging me down the stairs, I waited in his office in the back of the gym. A few minutes later he walked in with a clueless Cindy. He started yelling at her and I tried remaining calm.

"Heath, stop yelling at her." I wanted to believe with all my heart that he wouldn't go to so much trouble to prove his innocence if he wasn't. "Cindy. Please be truthful." My voice cracked, "My marriage is on the line. Did I call you yesterday to relay a message to Heath? Because when I called looking for him you told me he'd left a message for *me*."

She stood in silence and I couldn't get a good read on her. "Dammit Cindy. You told me that Lucy left me a message and that our appointment had been canceled. I'm losing my patience." He was pacing and then barked out, "Get out. You're fired."

Her chin began to quiver and I realized we were both crying for our loss; her job and my marriage. She looked to me as I wiped at my tears. She couldn't help, my marriage was in shambles. "Ok. I was, oh, God."

We both yelled at her, "Spit it out!"

"I was in the back with Jeff when the phone started ringing. By the time I made it up front it had already stopped.

When I walked past your office a few minutes later, I found Stella in there. She said she was getting the last of her things, then handed me your cell and said that you must've left it behind and how lucky for me she answered the gym phone. I didn't think anything of it. She handed me a post-it with the message I was supposed to give you."

"Fuck!"

"Oh God." I collapsed in the chair, my chest heaving as the tears continued to fall.

"I'm sorry. She scares me and she threatened to tell you and Will about Jeff and I. I don't want to lose my job."

"That's enough Cindy. Get back to work."

"So I still have a job?"

"For now. Now get out!"

She scurried out of the room and shut the door behind her. "I told you!" He started yelling at me about how I should've believed him and it just fueled my fire.

Standing, I walked toward the door. "If you think for one minute that's the apology I want to hear, you're wrong."

"Apology for what? I didn't do anything wrong."

"Stella may have set us up, but you were still naked with her when I found you two. You expect me to believe nothing happened? You have a history."

"Not like the history I have with you. She's nothing. And yes, I expect you to believe me. I'm your husband."

"What about the paperwork? You're not my match. If I believe you and we put this behind us, can you live with that? Because I can't live with you continually doubting yourself. You either believe we belong together or you don't." He didn't say anything and after a moment of complete silence, I bit out, "Was this your plan all along?" He just stared back at me blankly and shook his head as if he didn't know what I was referring to. "Well, you succeeded."

I left. I took his silence for his answer, that he couldn't live with it and had no idea what he'd done to me. I wanted him to fight for me and it seemed when I thought he would, he'd just stand down. I didn't even know what the paperwork would reveal, but I was terrified to find out and it didn't seem to matter regardless. I needed him to want and need me. If we were going to make it, he had to fight for me, for us. I was back in our room and the tears began flowing freely, again, unable to stop them I just let them fall as I threw my belongings into my bag.

"Succeeded at what?" I began mumbling to myself. How could he not know what he did? "LUCY!"

His hand touched my arm and I flinched away from him, warning him to stay away. He took a step toward me and I shoved him back, yelling, "You know what you did. Was this just another game for you? 'Let's get Lucy to fall in love with me, again, only this time she'll know it's me the whole time'." I was still pulling items from drawers still rambling. "Congrats. My heart is in pieces, AGAIN, because of you."

"Lucy. What did you say?"

My head jerked up at him and my hands went to my hips. "You heard me. Just leave me alone. I'll be gone soon enough and you can get on with your life of breaking hearts."

I'd turned away from him, unsure what to do next. I felt the heat of his body behind me, knowing he was only centimeters away. Goosebumps ran down my spine as his fingers ran through the back of my hair. I'd never wanted to wrap my arms around him so badly. Of course my urge to physically hurt him was just as prevalent.

"Lucy. You fell in love with me?" I could only manage a sharp intake of breath, mixed with a growl. Like he didn't know. "Does that mean you don't love me anymore?"

Was he that dense? Turning to face him, I came nose to chest with him. I took a step back so I could look into his eyes. Wiping the tears off my cheeks, I accused him of being an idiot.

Shoving at his chest with all I had, he barely stumbled back. "No, I don't love you anymore! Is that what you want to hear?" He seemed confused. "Of course I love you, but…" I lost my train of thought as his lips curled up into a smile.

"But what?" His hands wrapped around each of my forearms and pulled me closer.

"But I can't be with you when you don't feel the same. When you won't fight for me. I don't need your pity."

"Pity! I don't pity you, Lucy." I couldn't bear to look at him. "I'm here, fighting for you the only way I know how. I can't lose you. I don't care about the paperwork." His finger came under my chin, requesting me to speak, he pleaded, "Say it again." My eyes narrowed as I tried to figure out what it was he wanted me to say. "Tell me you love me, Lucy."

Shaking my head, I pleaded with him, "Please don't. It hurts too much if you don't feel the same." His eyes became fierce and I gave in, though I couldn't look at him while I said it. "I love you." He didn't say anything. Not able to resist, I looked up into his chocolate eyes to find them smiling at me. "All I wanted was a small piece of your heart."

"You have more than a small piece. You have it all. I love you, Lucy." My expression showed my confusion, I was sure of it. Leaning down, he put his forehead to mine and repeated his sentiment. "I love you."

"But, I don't understand. When you didn't show up to our session I thought for sure that was your way of saying you didn't want to stay married anymore."

"You know why I didn't show up and I'm not mentioning her name again. I'll admit I thought for sure you'd want to end things. I don't think I'll ever believe that you want me."

My chest became tight and I was struggling to breathe, "So, I, you want to…"

His expression became concerned as I clutched at my chest. "Lucy, what's wrong?"

Panting and gasping for breath, I cried, "It hurts, I can't breathe."

Guiding me to sit down, he managed to calm me down, taking deep breaths with me. Once I was breathing somewhat normal, he asked, "You've been having panic attacks a lot lately."

"Only around you, it seems." He kissed my forehead and pulled me into his side. "Heath?"

"Yes?"

"So, you still want to stay married? No matter what the paperwork says?"

Pushing me back slightly, he glued the pieces of my heart back together with one statement. "I never wanted to *not* stay married, Lucy. I meant what I said that day." Fingering the charm that hung from my neck, "I'm your anchor and you're my home." I'd forgotten it still hung around my neck. "Always have been, always will be." Wiping the last remaining tears from my cheeks, he confessed, "I was afraid to tell you how I felt before knowing if you felt it, too. Now I know. I love you."

Smiling, I whimpered, "I love you, too."

His kiss started slow and soft, but soon we were breathless and clawing at one another. I needed to feel him inside me, beside me, and all over me. He was my match, regardless of what the paperwork said. He was meant to be mine and I was meant to be his. He was mine, my one and only. My love.

~ CHAPTER 31 ~

~ HEATH ~

The last twenty four hours surely had grey hair sprouting all over my head. I was exhausted from all the emotions. The thought of losing Lucy all because that bitch was determined to ruin my life had me reeling. The only thing I was guilty of was not giving her my heart. How could I when it'd always belonged to Lucy? I hoped Stella found someone to make her happy, but at the same time I believed karma had better plans in store for her.

Lucy stood in my arms, having just bared her soul to me, and mine to her. I loved her, more than she could possibly know. It wasn't easy for me to say. I think part of me had felt it and known it for years, having kept it bottled up for so long. It was easier to keep it hidden away, but the weight that was lifted from me when I finally told her was liberating.

Cupping her face I looked at her. Her eyes were closed as her hands clung to my waist. Kissing her nose, I whispered, "Why don't you get comfortable? I'll be right back."

Her eyes flew open in protest. "Don't go."

Chuckling, I reassured her, "I'm not leaving. I'll be right back." She let out a breath as I added, "I expect you on the bed and waiting for me when I come back in here." Tilting her head, the look in her eyes that called to me like a siren, she just nodded her head and I was surprised at her lack of rebuttal.

Valentine's Day had come and gone and we'd agreed to not celebrate it until after the appointment with Dr. Phillips. I still couldn't get over my idiocy. It'd been so easy for me to assume the message I got from Cindy was legit. I'd gotten Lucy a gift and it was in my glove box waiting.

Once in my car, I sat and opened the small box. It was simple and understated, but timeless. I prayed she'd like it. Making my way back upstairs, with the box in my pocket, I heard music coming from the bedroom. I recognized *Someday* by Nickelback and assumed she was playing one of the CDs I'd made her years earlier.

Walking through our bedroom door, I was stopped in my tracks. She was laying on her side in the middle of the bed in nothing but her bra and panties. With her head propped up, resting on her hand, she appeared to be lost in thought and hadn't seen me yet. I could stare at her this way forever. The black lace strap of the white bra had fallen off her shoulder and she was fingering the lace of her panties at her hip.

Staring at her, I scanned her body several times. "Kind of a somber song considering we're celebrating."

She jumped slightly and smiled up at me. "I like listening to them. Kinda feel like I'm rediscovering a part of you, a part of our youth that I missed out on." I closed the door and came closer to the bed. *Here Without You* by 3 Doors Down started. "You know whenever I'd hear this song, I'd think of you too?"

Crawling onto the bed, I confessed, "I dreamed about you all the time."

She moved to her back and welcomed my body as it covered hers. I sang the words to her as her hands ran over my face and shoulders. Her hands pulled my shirt over my head as I kicked off my shoes.

"It's only you and me from here on out."

"I have something for you." She smiled and waited as I pulled the box from my front pant pocket. Handing her the box, I prayed she'd like it.

She opened it and put a hand on her chest, "Oh, Heath..."

"Do you like it?"

"Heath, I love it. It's so timeless, like us." She pulled me down for a kiss without slipping it out of the box.

Pulling back, "Make sure it fits."

She handed me the box and urged me on, "You do it." Taking it from the box, I slid the ring on her finger, placing it next to her wedding band. "It's perfect." Her eyes met mine, "You're perfect."

We took our time that night. Slow and steady, hard and fast, we did it all. Nothing and no one would ever be able to change my love for this amazing woman. She was right. What we had spanned more than two decades and ran deeper than anyone but us could imagine. I prayed God would grant us a dozen more decades together. My only regret was that I hadn't fought for her sooner. She taught me things I didn't think I needed to learn.

Glancing at the photo on our night stand, I smiled. My mother had given us an album full of pictures from our childhood as a Christmas gift. We had the biggest laugh over one of me, Will, and Lucy as a toddler. Lucy assumed that I was the one making a dirty face at the beautiful blonde haired toddler, when in fact it was Will. In the picture Will and I are about four years old and Lucy had just started learning to walk. Her arms outstretched, with a big grin on her face as she made her way toward me. Will behind her with the look of annoyance on his face. I don't think anyone would've guessed twenty five years ago how telling that photo would be.

But the one Lucy had framed was my favorite. It was of her and me standing on the beach holding hands. I loved that photo more than words could say.

Several hours later as we laid naked in each other's arms, the CDs playing over and over again, my favorite came on. "You know the night we watched this movie I told you I loved you." She leaned up and looked at me in disbelief. "Don't worry, you were asleep and I knew that when I said it."

"What were you so afraid of?" I shrugged my shoulders. "I'm sorry I ever let you doubt how I felt, how I feel about you." A tear slipped from her eye and I wiped it away. "I've said some horrible things to you. Can you forgive me?"

"Lucy." I shushed her, kissing her forehead. "I can forgive you. All you have to do is taste my Heath bar."

Giggling, she smacked my arm and chastised me. "Way to ruin the moment."

"Ow!" I laced my fingers with hers before pinning her underneath me. "The moment will never be ruined." She accepted my kiss and soon her body was arching up into mine, seeking me out.

"I have a confession, too." Pulling back I looked at her. "I never opened the paperwork."

"Wait, but you said..."

"I lied. I was hurt and wanted to hurt you back." I knelt up and she pulled me back down. "You're my match, no matter what that paperwork says. I only want you."

"Burn it. I want that paperwork burned."

"Consider it done."

"You're mine and that's all that matters."

Smiling and holding my face in her hands she stilled her eyes on mine. "I see you, Heathcliff Daniel Kerrigan. I know who you are. Your breath is my life and you're the only one who knows who I am. You own me, always have."

My heart imploded with her words. I knew which song she was referring to and knew that all the pain and waiting we'd gone through was worth it. She was mine and she finally understood that I'd always been hers.

~ EPILOGUE ~

~ HEATH ~

The week after Independence Day, we sat on the beach at the lake house. Our families had all been up there and had left earlier in the day. The next few days were ours and ours alone. She was reading a book as I tried to not be distracted by her figure in a bikini. Toes curling in the sand, I took a swig of my beer and dropped my head back against the chair.

"Get your head out of the gutter, Heathcliff."

"How do you know it's in the gutter? You're the one reading that smut."

Eyeing me mischievously, she retorted, "It's damn good smut!"

"Hmph, well, it's taking away from my smutty time with you."

Setting down her e-reader she smirked, "But it's giving me so many good ideas of how to be *smuttier* with you."

"Well in that case, read on." Before I knew it, she was in my lap and attempting to tickle me. "When are you going to give up? I'm not ticklish."

"Never. And yes you are."

Her hand reached between my legs and found the one spot that always sent me reeling. High up on my inner thigh was about the only place I was ticklish.

Prying her hand away as I squirmed she giggled when I started tickling her in return. After a few minutes of messing around she wrapped her arms around my neck and burrowed into me.

"I love it here and I love you."

"Love you, too, baby." Running my hands up and down her back I couldn't help but think about little Lucys and Heathcliffs running the beach with us. "Have you thought anymore about having a baby?" Our families—mostly our mothers—had been relentless the past week wanting to know when we were going to have kids.

I felt her take a deep breath as she turned her head. Talking into my neck, she revealed, "I think about babies all the time, but we're still so young. We have time." Sighing she reminded me, "You said once you weren't ready to share me with our baby. I feel the same way. What about you? Have you thought about what I said?"

I wasn't going to push her about having a baby and I was happy to keep her all to myself, for now. But I also loved the idea of her pregnant and couldn't wait for that step in our journey. As to her question, I *had* thought about it a lot.

"You really think we should open a gym up here? It's a long drive."

"I love it up here. O's taking the reins of the Montrose gym and can help out with the others too. We could run one up here and go down there on weekends."

"What about your friends and your job?"

Leaning back, she smiled, "They'll always be there and I can find a part time hygienist job up here if need be."

Observing her, I was proud to call her mine. "Ok. I'll talk to Will. We'll start scouting locations."

"Really?"

"Yes. I'm sure mom and dad won't mind us staying here until we get a gym up and off the ground!"

She jumped off my lap and did a cartwheel in the sand as I laughed at her. Standing to join her, she jumped on my back as we walked down the beach, her clinging to me.

"Heath," she sweetly whispered in my ear, "about the baby..." That got my attention, "let's go practice!"

"You just wanna taste my heath bar." She pinched my nipple as we laughed. "Who am I to deny you?" I carried her all the way back to the house where we practiced the rest of the day and night, only stopping to refuel.

Lucy Roberts Kerrigan. I stared at her as she slept while music played softly. *All I Want* by Dawn Golden echoed my feelings.

She stirred and her eyes barely opened, "Stop staring at me and go to sleep."

She rolled over and curled her back into my chest. Memories of us as kids filtered through my mind. I'd always been enamored with her, but it wasn't until that summer eleven years ago when I'd fully fallen for her. It'd taken all our trust, honor, and love to reach the place we were at now. And I wouldn't change a thing. She was my world and the only thing I needed in this life was her love.

THE END...FOR NOW

TRUST HONOR & LOVE
HELPED LUCY AND HEATH
FIND EACH OTHER.

WHICH KERRIGAN
BROTHER
WILL BE NEXT?

BODY HEART SOUL
BLIND VOWS
VOLUME 2

PLAYLIST

Hollow Moon (Bad Wolf) by Awolnation

Me & U by Cassie

Believe by Mumford & Sons

The Words by Christina perri

Dear Future Husband by Meghan Trainor

History In The Making by Darius Rucker

The Reason by Hoobastank

Only You by Matthew Perryman

Bad Girl by Avril Lavigne

Animals by Chris Call

Ride by SoMo

She Will Be Loved by Maroon 5

What Kind Of Man by Florence & The Machine

Iris by The Goo Goo Dolls

You by The Pretty Reckless

Line Of Fire by The Veronicas

Just A Little Bit Of Your Heart by Ariana Grande

Someday by Nickelback

Here Without You by 3 Doors Down

All I Want by Dawn Golden

MORE FROM J.M. WITT

THE ANCHORED HEARTS SERIES

Letting Go (Vol. 1) *

Hiding Away (Vol. 1.5) *

Letting Go of You (Vol. 2) *

Fading Away (Vol. 2.5) *

Letting Go of Us (Vol. 3) *

Concrete Soul (Vol. 4) * * * (Paul's story)

Untitled (Vol. 5) * * * (Smith's story)

Drifting Away (Vol. 6) * * * (Cal & Jane: whole series epilogue)

THE BLIND VOWS SERIES

Trust, Honor, Love

Body, Heart, Soul * * *

THE CONVICTED SERIES

Publisher: Booktrope

Convicted Heart * * *

Convicted Fidelity * * *

Convicted Justice * * *

Out Now = *   Coming Soon = * * *

ABOUT THE AUTHOR

J.M. resides in Metro Detroit, MI with her husband and four young children.

Always wanting to write romance novels, she followed her dreams after having baby #4, who may or may not be the spawn of Christian Grey!

She hopes you'll enjoy more than a good book, but have an experience.

You can find her at

www.jmwittbooks.com

Twitter @wittymomauthor

www.facebook.com/jmwittbooks

www.ingramcontent.com/pod-product-compliance
Lightning Source LLC
Chambersburg PA
CBHW060404180626
46817CB00007B/2509